WHERE REASONS END

A NOVEL

———

YIYUN LI

PENGUIN BOOKS

PENGUIN BOOKS

UK | USA | Canada | Ireland | Australia
India | New Zealand | South Africa

Penguin Books is part of the Penguin Random House group of companies
whose addresses can be found at global.penguinrandomhouse.com.

Penguin
Random House
UK

First published in the United States of America by Random House,
an imprint of Penguin Random House LLC 2019
First published in Great Britain by Hamish Hamilton 2019
Published in Penguin Books 2020
001

Grateful acknowledgement is made to the following for permission
to reprint previously published material:
"Argument" from *Poems* by Elizabeth Bishop © 2011. Published by Chatto & Windus.
Reprinted by permission of The Random House Group Limited.
An excerpt from "Days" from *The Complete Poems of Philip Larkin* by Philip Larkin.
Reprinted by permission of Faber and Faber Ltd.
"This Solitude of Cataracts" from *Collected Poems* by Wallace Stevens.
Reprinted by permission of Faber and Faber Ltd.

Typeset by Jouve (UK), Milton Keynes
Printed and bound in Great Britain by Clays Ltd, Elcograf S.p.A.

A CIP catalogue record for this book is available from the British Library

ISBN: 978-0-241-98518-2

www.greenpenguin.co.uk

For Dapeng and James
and in memory of Vincent Kean Li (2001–2017)

Days that cannot bring you near
or will not,
Distance trying to appear
something more than obstinate,
argue argue argue with me
endlessly
neither proving you less wanted nor less dear.

Distance: Remember all that land
beneath the plane;
that coastline
of dim beaches deep in sand
stretching indistinguishably
all the way,
all the way to where my reasons end?

Days: And think
of all those cluttered instruments,
one to a fact,
canceling each other's experience;
how they were
like some hideous calendar
"Compliments of Never & Forever, Inc."

The intimidating sound
of these voices
we must separately find
can and shall be vanquished:
Days and Distance disarrayed again
and gone
both for good and from the gentle battleground.

—Elizabeth Bishop, "Argument"

Contents

WHERE
REASONS
END

1

Do Not Let Mother Dear Find Us

Mother dear, Nikolai said.

I was surprised. He used to only call me that when I wasn't paying attention. But here I was, holding on to my attentiveness because that was all I could do for him now. I've never told you how much I loved you calling me that, I said.

What did you call Grandma?

When I was your age? Mamita, I said.

That was endearing, he said.

You have to get the name right when you find the person hard to endear, I said. Endear, I thought, what an odd word. Endear. Endure. En-dear. In-dear. Can you out-dear someone?

And fancy seeing you here, Nikolai said.

One of us made this happen, I said.

I blame you.

I laughed. Ever so like you, I said. I then explained the liberty I had taken to get myself here. For one thing, I had made time irrelevant.

I could be sixteen like you are, I said, or twenty-two, or thirty-seven, or forty-four.

I would rather you are not sixteen, he said.

Why not?

I don't want to feel the obligation to befriend you.

We can still be friends even if I am of another age.

I don't like making friends with older people. Besides, one can't really be friends with one's mother.

Can one not?

No. The essence of growing up is to play hide-and-seek with one's mother successfully, Nikolai said.

All children win, I said. Mothers are bad at seeking.

You did find me.

Not as your mother, I said. Don't you notice the sign there (though I knew he couldn't have—I had hung it up while talking with him): *Do not let mother dear find us.*

What are you then?

Oh, a runaway bunny like you. How else did we end up here?

Here, as I watched my neighbor leave, a box of fresh-baked chocolate cookies in my hands, was a place called nowhere. The rule is, somewhere tomorrow and somewhere yesterday—but never somewhere today.

I was neither the White Queen, who sets the rule, nor Alice, who declines to live by the rule. I was a generic parent grieving a generic child lost to an inexplicable tragedy. Already there were three clichés. I could wage my personal war against each one of them. Grieve: from Latin *gravare,* to burden, and *gravis,* grave, heavy. What kind of mother would consider it a burden to live in the vacancy left behind by a child? Explicate: from Latin *ex* (out) + *plicare* (fold), to unfold. But calling Nikolai's action inexplicable was like calling a migrant bird ending on a new continent lost. Who can say the vagrant doesn't have a reason to change the course of its flight? Nothing inexplicable for me—only I didn't want to explain: A mother's job is to enfold, not to unfold.

Tragedy: Now that is an inexplicable word. What was a goat song, after all, which is what tragedy seemed to mean originally?

Would you call it a tragedy yourself? I asked Nikolai. In the interim between talking with my neighbor and returning to this page, I realized the world might think I was becoming unhinged.

I was not. What I was doing was what I had always

been doing: writing stories. In this one the child Nikolai (which was not his real name, but a name he had given himself, among many other names he had used) and his mother dear meet in a world unspecified in time and space. It was not a world of gods or spirits. And it was not a world dreamed up by me; even my dreams were mundane and landlocked in reality. It was a world made up by words, and words only. No images, no sounds.

Would you call it a tragedy? he said.

I would only say it's sad. It's so sad I have no other adjectives left.

Adjectives are my guilty pleasure, he said.

I know. You may have to supply me some, I said. Which one word, I wondered, would he come up with to describe my nowhere-ness? Then it occurred to me that he wouldn't give me a word. No matter how much liberty I had taken in this world, I could not change the fact that I had made this meeting take place. It wasn't his choice so he was limited by my ability. I had no words but sadness.

Do you want me to feel sad for myself, too? Nikolai said.

I thought about the question. I didn't know the answer.

I'm not as sad as you think, he said. Not anymore.

I didn't need him to tell me that, but wouldn't it be good, my child, if you could still feel sad as I do, because then you could feel other things as I do, too? But I didn't say these words to him. Instead, I told him a story about my high school classmate's mother.

The woman grew up on an island in Indonesia. One day she climbed a coconut tree to pick a coconut for her little sister, and plunged from the tree. She did not die but lost most of her hearing from the accident. Later she became a pianist and taught in a conservatory. You had to shout into her ear for her to hear you. I'd never seen her play piano or teach. It was a mystery to me how she could do either.

Beethoven was deaf, too, Nikolai said.

Only later in his life. She was deaf since she was seven.

Was her life more of a tragedy than Beethoven's?

No, of course not, I said. The reason I was telling you the story was that I now remember she liked me a lot.

As I was talking, more details about the woman and her daughter came to me, the first time I had thought of them in thirty years. My friend was a wild, unruly girl of sixteen, with hair cut by herself, unevenly in the back and front. She failed the college entrance exam and we drifted apart. I had heard she had become a freelance photographer.

The friend's mother liked to keep me next to her, feeding me sugared citrus and tea when a group of us visited their apartment. She and I rarely talked, but we smiled at each other often. She was an odd woman, half a head taller than her daughter, who was among the tallest in my class, and she was helplessly quiet in front of her daughter, who often joked that I was a perfect companion for her mother.

Not only this friend's mother, I said. Back then I happened to be liked by all my friends' parents.

I am not liked by all my friends' parents, Nikolai said with some pride.

I know. I admire you for that, I said. All the same, they still cry for you.

It doesn't matter now, he said.

Had it been me at sixteen, many of my friends' parents would have thought it an inexplicable tragedy. But that knowledge would not have made the world less bleak for me. I hadn't thought about my friend's mother for decades. Other than a few facts about her life and her smile, I didn't know her at all, nor she me.

I suppose you're right, I said. Still, I wish you knew how much you are missed by many people.

Mommy, Nikolai said, and the way he said it almost made me weep. Mommy, you know that's a cliché.

What if life could be saved by clichés? What if life must be lived by clichés? Somewhere tomorrow and somewhere yesterday—never somewhere today but cliché-land.

You promised that you would understand, Nikolai said.

Understanding I had promised him. And other things, too: a house in the woods, a kitchen with sunlight, many new recipes, rights to my books—after you die I want the rights to the books you've written, but only the good ones, he had said to me at nine. Yet all these promises were as inadequate as love, promise and love being two anchors of cliché-land.

That doesn't change how sad I am, I said.

But you wouldn't want people to feel sad all the time if you were me.

I was almost you once, and that's why I have allowed myself to make up this world to talk with you. Sadness one can live with, but sadness is a helpless garrison against the blindness of tragedy. A mother and a child cannot be contemporaries at any given age, and for that reason my sixteen-year-old self could not befriend yours. Each refusing to be saved, we could not save each other when young. Older—and you were still young—I was the White Queen who put up the sign. *Do not let mother dear find us.* You were the one better at hiding.

2

Waylaid by Days

Now we have our own rules, I said. A step toward somewhere, isn't it?

I didn't say how it had made breathing possible. Life, if not lived, is carried by automatic actions, breathing an inevitable one among them. Once at a party someone asked what were the qualities in other people that set one off. I said imprecision.

As though we haven't always lived by our own rules, Nikolai said. His tone, I imagined, would be the same as when he had once said—after I questioned what other mothers would think of his outfit, unsuitable for a concert he was going to—you don't even care what others think of you.

Have we always lived by our own rules? But more than the question, I was confused by the tense we used.

Queries had been made, and advice given, regarding in what tense I spoke about Nikolai. Yet what makes *was* different from *is, has been* from *will be*? Timeless is this world we are making, tenseless its language.

Rules are set to be broken, he said.

Deadlines are set to be missed, I said. Deadline as a word used to fascinate me, a word that connects time and space and death with such absoluteness.

Promises are made not to be kept, he said.

Love is made not to last, I said. A contestable statement, though he chose not to argue. Love was the word we had used at his leave-taking, he knowing it was final, I sensing it was the case. But between sensing and knowing there were seven hours and four states. Only today did I register that people often in their condolence letters called the loss unfathomable. The distance at the moment of loss could be calculated: 189,200 fathoms. (What does it matter that fathom is no longer used to measure from here to there? To obsolete is to let age, from which death is exempted.)

Not clear, though, is how to fathom time: from a moment to . . . Can forever be the other end point?

But why does it bother you if you insist time does not apply to us anymore? Nikolai said. Omniscience was taken for granted in this world where we met now, but omniscience I let only him claim. You're breaking your own rules, he said.

Because time still confines and confuses me, I said.

Poor you, he said. Waylaid by time.

Waylay, I said. I've never used it in my writing.

No offense, but you don't have an expansive vocabulary.

Luckily my mind is not limited by my vocabulary, I said. (In my head I used the same tone that I had used when Nikolai had introduced me to his kindergarten class: My mom is an immigrant so she speaks English with an accent. Thank you my dear, I had said then, but I still make a living by writing in English.)

He turned quiet. I understood. Who wants to hear a mother boast about herself?

I turned quiet, too. I was in a subway car. Only a few weeks ago, Nikolai had asked me if it was always this loud underground. We had been on the way to meet my friend, as I was doing today. I can't live in New York, he had said then. I can't afford to lose my hearing.

It occurred to me, when I remembered his words now, that I had never paid attention to the noise. I had known I was not sensitive to colors, but to sounds also?

How have I lived so blindly and deafly? I said. Perhaps he had gained knowledge to explain that to me.

He did not reply. He was eavesdropping on a man and a woman standing next to me. I was late to their story. They were talking about a boy who had killed himself the week before, the son of a mutual acquaintance.

Seventeen, the man said. Can you believe it?

Oh my god, the woman said. I read it in the papers. I thought to myself, Someone's grandson.

Imagine being woken up by that phone call, the man said. How can anyone believe it's real?

I waited for Nikolai to say something. He would not defend the other boy, I knew that. They each had their own reasons to make a decision that looked similar only to those wanting an explanation. But I wondered if he would say something clever, that people's sympathy and callousness are like two hands wringing over someone else's disaster. Or, would he poke fun at them on my behalf? Of course you knew it was real right away, did you not? he would say. How can anyone ask a question starting with that silly phrase *How can anyone*.

But he did not say anything.

Isn't it strange that her first thought was someone's

grandson, I said after the man and the woman exited the car.

She just met her first grandchild, Nikolai said.

I had missed that part. We went into the tunnel. I wondered if the noise still bothered him.

I can hear you fine, he said.

Oh, I said. There is one thing that troubles me. I can't find all those poems you wrote.

Or those I will write.

Touché, I said. I then explained that someone had asked if I had enough of his poetry to make a chapbook.

Chap, ChapStick, chapman, chapbook, he said. All sound small to me. Like you're going to make—what did they call it in the old time—a miniature of my mind.

How I loved that his ambition and conceit would remain as young as he was. They would be handmade, like what you did in bookbinding, I said.

Those notebooks have blank pages.

Not all books have to be blank, I said. Everyone agrees you are a beautiful poet.

Ha, from reading those doodlings I sent you when I was a kid? he said. You don't understand poetry.

You as me, your mother, or you as the world?

You as my mommy, he said. Nikolai might be the

only sixteen-year-old to still call his mother Mommy. No offense, but your taste is not to be trusted, he said.

I laughed. He had said the same thing when we had been in a shop in Edinburgh, choosing woolen and cashmere scarves for him.

Those scarves are mine now, I said.

Like pass-me-ups?

You don't mind my wearing them?

I haven't worn them so they're not mine yet. But I do mind, he said, you or anyone reading my poetry.

I told him about an exhibition of Philip Larkin I had seen in England. There were covers of Larkin's journals, the insides taken out and burned in a fireplace the day after his death.

I applaud that as much as you do, Nikolai said.

The key is to have someone you trust agree to live longer, I said.

But I can't entrust my poetry to anyone, he said.

I thought about the people in the world who would all live longer than he. Would I trust any of them? Would I trust myself?

It's not your fault, he said.

If you use fault in the sense of wrongdoing, I said, no, it's not. But the root of the word fault came from *to disappoint, to deceive.*

Nikolai waited for me to go on. He was not often this patient in hearing me out.

Who can say to love doesn't also mean to disappoint and to deceive? I said.

Those who disappoint or deceive don't always do so from love, he said.

That, my child, doesn't help a parent. If the job description of parenting, I thought, had come with the requirement to disappoint and to deceive, how many of us would have set out with guiltless hope in the first place?

Or hopeless guilt? he said. But you've decided that in this world we don't abide by the rules that bind a child and a parent.

The line between self-deception and willpower is often blurred, I said.

I inherited both from you, didn't I? he said. It's not your fault, though.

Willpower was among his qualities I would remember. When he was in fifth grade, he had had trouble sleeping. Later he told me, when we were arguing, that whatever we had suggested had been of little help. I went to bed at nine and willed my body to stay still and my brain to stop thinking, he had said. That was how I solved my insomnia and that will always be the way I solve my problems. I can't rely on anyone but my own willpower.

The line between willpower and arrogance is blurred, too, I said.

That, unfortunately, cannot be changed, he said. Give will some power and it turns blind. Just as people with power become so full of themselves they can't see their own toes.

But then when does willpower see?

Willpower doesn't have eyes to see, he said. Wishy-washiness has eyes, though. Too many. Like Argos.

Nikolai used to call me wishy-washy because he had liked the sound of it.

We can't then let willpower lead us, I said.

You can't, he said.

But how else does one live if not by willpower, when day after day after day after day a child hides himself? I read him a stanza from a Larkin poem:

What are days for?
Days are where we live.
They come, they wake us.
Time and time over.
They are to be happy in:
Where can we live but days?

Days are not the only place where we live, Nikolai said.

Time is not the only place where we live, I said. Days are.

I don't have to have days to live now.

And yet I have to live in days, I said.

I'm sorry, he said.

Days: the easiest possession, requiring only automatic participation. The days he had refused would come, one at a time. Neither my allies nor my enemies, they would wait, every daybreak, with their boundless patience and indifference, seeing if they could turn me into a friend or an enemy to myself.

Never apologize, I said, for what you have let go.

3

The Trespassers

I've been trying to find that poem by Elizabeth
Bishop, I said. Remember, the one you wrote about?

I don't, Nikolai said.

The first week of sixth grade, I said. You wrote how
the poem made you realize memory turned the places
we traveled to into different colors for you.

Purplish gray for Croatia, he said.

Yes!

Gold and silver for Paris.

Some odd choice for Berlin, I said. Some odder
choice for Beijing. What colors were they?

I don't remember.

Which poem is it?

I don't remember that, either.

What are the rules of knowing and remembering
for him now? For weeks I had been reading through

Bishop's poems, but none of them looked like the right one. Could he not name the poem, I thought, unfettered by memory?

Unfettered, he said. You chose the wrong word.

I looked up the word. He must have acquired a dictionary's worth of knowledge.

If memory were a fetter, he said, many people would envy me.

Why?

Each day they live makes the fetter more unbreakable than the day before.

What if, I thought, that is life's necessity?

Still, I said, aren't you able to know the poem even if you can't remember?

It doesn't work the way you imagined.

Why not?

Something in the past, he said, and so specific. No, knowing is not about that.

In other words, I said, omniscience does not apply retrospectively. I kept having to refrain from saying: where you are.

Dilemmas are ubiquitous, he said, wherever you are.

Di-lemmas: two assumptions. Omniscience and memory: both questionable.

If one has to choose? I asked.

Memory is like eye color, he said. You always have it.

Yet one can choose to shut one's eyes, I thought.

That doesn't change your eye color, he said. Omniscience is like the ability to write poetry. Not all people are born with it.

Can one not acquire it? I asked.

Can you write poetry?

I thought about the question hard. No, I conceded. But I do like to use omniscient narrators in fiction.

Ha. That sounds like my friends who bring store-bought cookies to the bake sale.

I feel unfairly judged, I said.

There is a perfection in omniscience that you don't have and don't understand, he said.

Or I don't believe in perfection?

It's lazy-minded of you to say you don't believe in something that you don't understand.

I thought about the things I didn't understand. These days they often came back to Nikolai. Before daybreak I had remembered a little song he had made up when he was six and his little brother, J., was three, which they sang in tandem when having a bath to-gether:

Happy-go-lucky fish
   Happy-go-lucky fish
Message-in-a-bottle fish
   Message-in-a-bottle fish
Rubber-ducky fish
   Rubber-ducky fish

You know it meant nothing, right? Nikolai said. I made it up to amuse ourselves because you never got us out of the bathtub in time.

How would I know it meant nothing, I thought, when something and nothing seem to be walking hand in hand now, identical twins dressed in each other's outfits. The song, having circled in my head long enough, had acquired an indecipherability. All things indecipherable felt as though they possessed an inner logic.

Even if it means something, why not make that something into nothing? he said.

How?

Oh, I thought grownups are good at it. If someone asks you, Is there something wrong?, to be a good-mannered and considerate person you should answer, Thank you for asking but nothing is wrong. You don't say, Thank you for asking but nothing is right. People would freak out if you said that, and if they freaked out, what would you say? Oh, please don't worry, even though nothing is right, nothing is left, either.

You make my head swim, I complained. I have to write your words down to understand their meaning.

You're being silly, like English teachers always asking us to look for metaphors in the text, Nikolai said.

Life is not lived by metaphors, we said together. He had heard that first when he had to sit through my teaching for five hours. He was four, and lay under a long table, slowly but persistently rolling from one end to the other and then back. The next day he said I had been mean when I said, Sometimes nothing is wrong with a story but that it's boring.

When you made up that song, did you have a rubber duck or a rubber fish in the bathtub? I asked. Or both?

Neither, he said. How can you let your imagination be so limited?

Not imagination, I said, but one wants to make certain that the detail is right.

Why does it matter?

True, I thought. Right or wrong, the song had kept me awake but dreading to rise and meet the day.

Remember what you used to say to me? Nikolai said. Proportion, proportion, proportion.

I had also said to him, Patience, patience, patience; perspective, perspective, perspective.

Peter Piper picked a peck of pickled peppers, he said.

I laughed. I was always in awe that he could say anything as fast as humanly possible.

As fast as inhumanly possible, that's what you should rather use in your thinking now, he said.

Of course not.

Why not, if you make so much ado about precision? A misused adverb is worse than an adverb, he said.

I used to edit adverbs out of his writing. I had expected our arguments to continue, but to argue about adverbs? Oh, please, I said.

Fine, he said.

I only meant that we have so much to say to each other, I said, rather than quibbling.

Do we really?

Am I presumptuous to think that our conversation has not been interrupted despite life's finickiness? What we have is finickier than life. Any disturbance would disperse this—and what is this, in any case? Not dreaming, not hallucinating, not running away together, not running away separately, but running into each other constantly. Finding a way to be when it is difficult, and impossible, to be—is it for him, too?

I'm sorry. I didn't mean to shut you off, I said.

He remained quiet. I had made a mistake. Even arguing for the sake of arguing was better than dead silence.

What's disproportional about me now? I said, trying to regain his attention, but he didn't speak. Is that how a mother loses a child? Is that how any person loses any person, by not understanding the treachery of words, or worse, by thinking one can conquer that with precision? Silence is the best defense and the best offense. What happens when one counters silence with silence, like the ironsmith in the Chinese fable who brags about having cast the strongest armor that would shield against the fiercest spear, and the fiercest spear that would pierce the strongest armor? We would both be quiet ever after.

See how you let your mind be carried away to the wrong place, he said.

I was relieved. How so?

Would you have found me had I decided to remain

lost to you? Would you have received a word from me had I decided that not speaking suited me well?

True, I said.

But you decide to remain wimpy.

A mother like me, I wanted to protest, is far from wimpy. But all I could think about was the newest release of *Diary of a Wimpy Kid,* which he would never read now. Nikolai was way past the age but he had once commented that growing up on a series of books meant the obligation to always read the next installment.

See what I mean? he said. Never again. Every time you think, you end a thought on that phrase. What's the big deal if it's never again?

Nothing can be called a big deal now, I thought. If every moment is the curtain call to the previous moment, yes, we can throw up our hands and say, What's the big deal? Where is the climax of this play? But big deals and climaxes only form a vacuum cleaner of time. It's the small deals and the nothing deals that shatter time into ragged pieces. Days, strewn with expected and unexpected moments, did not offer a shortcut by saying, What's the big deal? The day before, I was packing his clothes for a move to a new house. Among them was an oversize white shirt with the *Wimpy Kid* book title in Norwegian, which I had brought back from a publisher in Oslo. For a few years he had worn that as a pajama shirt. I had not paid attention to it while packing because there were other shirts, more meaningful, with better stories to tell, but now it had regained its place to tell its own story. Every afternoon I waited in the middle of a block, where I used to wait for Nikolai and his brother to come from two directions. On some rare days I was disciplined enough to face only one direction. Other days I turned around. Turning around was not a mistake, because no lesson could be learned. Turning around always brought a moment of haziness to my thought: There was no reason that the tree-lined street would not bring Nikolai back again, unhurried as a gray heron.

See, now you think like everyone else: How can anyone . . .

How can anyone—I said—what?

How can anyone believe that one day he was here and the next day he was gone?

Yet how can one, I thought. How can one know a fact without accepting it? How can one accept a person's choice without questioning it? How can one question without reaching a dead end? How much reaching does one have to do before one finds another end beyond the dead end? And if there is another end beyond the dead end, it cannot be called dead, can it?

How good you are, Nikolai said, at befuddling yourself.

Fuddled, muddled, befuddled, I said. Every time you say something I have to turn to the dictionary. Every word has ten more definitions I have missed.

Nobody says you have to know all the definitions.

What if one could only make sense with those missing definitions.

Most people won't bother themselves with that, you know.

Most—I said, and then, to be less generalizing, I revised myself—many people don't have to go to this extreme as I do so as not to lose someone. I thought about what people said, that there are ways to keep the dead alive, that it's our love and memory that carry them with us. But was that enough for Nikolai? Any lesser way would only make him vanish again. He had outwitted many people. There was no reason he would not do it again.

Sounds like trespassing to me, Nikolai said.

My trespassing in your life? I said. Just the day before I had decorated a room in the new house, which we called Nikolai's room, with a sign he had made for his bedroom in our old house in California. STAY OUT.

And the part of your mind where you shouldn't enter, he said.

Does one have to stay out of part of one's own mind? I asked.

If you don't want to be out of your mind entirely, he said.

Do you stay clear from where you shouldn't be in your mind?

Do you mean: Do I, or did I?

It makes no difference, I said.

If I'm the trespasser of my own mind I've acquitted myself, he said.

Then I shall acquit myself, too.

Don't trespass in the first place, he said.

Too late, I said. To love is to trespass.

To live, too, he said. How can anyone not see it that way?

4

Then the Button Came Undone

Why, you've been quiet, Nikolai said.

I had been. I couldn't find words just yet.

Bad day? he said.

I realized then that not all rules of this world were clear to me. Did he go everywhere I went, see everything I saw?

Not really, he said. Not always.

Even omniscience is limited, I thought. So your ability to read my thoughts doesn't extend to the ability to see the physical world I traverse, I said.

It depends.

On what?

My mood.

Where are you when you're not in the mood to be here? I asked.

Here, which here?

I mean when you're not in the mood to talk with me, I said.

But that was not precise, either.

That's not for you to know, he said.

I had just driven past the corner of F—— and M——, where I used to drop him off in the morning. I told him that. By accident, I said. There was a detour I didn't expect.

Where I last saw you, he said.

That line should be mine, I thought.

Mine, too, he said.

Why, you're quiet again, he said after a long pause.

Some things are still harder for me than for you, I said.

Like what?

I thought about the eight hours between when I had dropped him off at the intersection and when he had died. Eight hours was a long time. What had happened would always be unknown to me.

Perhaps it's the least important thing to know? he said.

How many eight hours can be fit into a life? I had known Nikolai for sixteen years and twenty-two days. I had loved him longer. When he was an infant, I had worked in a hospital, and for the duration of the workday, longer than eight hours, he would refuse to take a drop from a bottle, and then would nurse every hour after I got off work, all night long. A six-week-old baby or a sixteen-year-old boy, unyielding to the point of extravagant intrepidity.

Still, I said, here's eight hours, something you know and I don't.

I wouldn't know what happens to your days most of the time, either, he said.

Mine, this, I said, is a different kind of not knowing.

Not knowing is not knowing, he said.

And not knowing must be close to what people call a wound. Along with wound are words like healing and scars. They are all bad analogies, the foundation of wishful thinking. Can one live, I thought, with a conclusion so fatally inconclusive?

The question should be, Does one want to? Nikolai said.

I remembered a story he had worked on in middle school, about a five-year-old boy named Nikolai. Uprooted by the 1917 Revolution, he and his mother fled St. Petersburg, accompanied by his nanny. They dressed him in a new coat, but neither woman talked while waiting for the train to leave the station.

He used to show me a page or two as he had finished them. I had not known what had led him to write the story. Nikolai—the boy in his story, the boy journeying to the unknown—sat in the train car and kept fingering a shiny brass button on his coat. His nanny told him not to do it, while the mother remained silent.

"Then the button came undone, and the coat was no longer new."

I remembered the chill when I had read the line. I remembered telling him a sentence like that would take him a long way if he decided to become a writer. He was twelve then, not quite trusting my words. He could never write as perfect a sentence as he wanted, he had replied, my admiration making him more dejected.

But it's true, he said now. Perfection is my only way of living.

Then the button came undone, and the coat was no longer new.

Nikolai—I said—I mean that boy in the story, he'd turn a hundred and five this year.

He's dead, he said. If that's not obvious enough.

When did he die? I asked. I had never seen the end of the story.

I didn't finish it, he said. But I suppose he didn't live past twelve or thirteen.

It was not the first time a boy had died in his stories. In fourth grade, a school project had led to a note of concern from the teacher, and queries from a few parents I had been friendly with.

They're only stories, he said. You write stories. You're making things up even at this moment.

Sometimes what you make up is realer than the real, I thought.

The dictionary would disagree with your statement, he said.

I looked up the word. Real, coming from *res,* fact, thing, and *realis,* relating to things.

What you make up is always unreality, he said. Relating to nothings.

Okay, I said.

Don't be crestfallen because you lost an argument, Nikolai said. Did you see any change there?

Where?

The corner that makes you sad.

A lot more leaves have fallen, I said.

There were already a lot of fallen leaves then.

I did not need him to remind me of that. I had seen them, the leaves on the ground, on a morning that was not yet autumn, and I had seen him hop over a pile, walking away. Since that day I had watched the trees shed their leaves for weeks but it never seemed to come to an end. Only in an O. Henry story does the last leaf take on an existential significance. Only in an O. Henry story does everything come with a poetic and tragic twist. The truth is, leaves are always falling. After a while they all look the same, the ones shuddering in the wind and the ones hurled around before they are cleaned up by blowers and mowers.

Blowers and mowers, Nikolai said. You need to try harder if you want to learn rhyming.

It occurred to me that he was indeed unable to see the physical world where I was. The leaves and the leaf-clearing rituals were abstract to him—he had not lived, since age three, in a place where leaves fell so profusely in one season. What else, which would have been merely new, became otherworldly to him? Snow and snow days, icicles under the eaves, crocuses that we had planned to plant together blooming in February, a cardinal knocking on the window with his head and beak—was it fondness or animosity toward its own reflection that made the red bird persist? Nikolai had only seen Steller's jays near our old house. They were confident birds, loud, territorial, always at war with the squirrels.

Since when have you begun to talk about nature? Nikolai asked. And all those small things.

Where else can one turn to but nature if one needs endless details to sustain oneself, I thought. Nature is not small, I said.

You weren't that interested in it.

I knew he had a point. The land I had traveled: The more intangible it is, the less hindered one feels, and the more invisible.

Still, I said, I've paid attention.

Attention out of disinterest or indifference, he said, is worse than inattention.

Touché, I said.

You're bad at looking and seeing, he said.

Looking, yes, I said. But seeing? There must be a difference between those two. Some people can look and look and look and look without seeing anything.

But you're claiming the opposite: seeing without having to look.

I thought about it. Just the day before I had seen a flock of birds take off from an open field to an overcast northern sky. Had I seen the scene before? Multiple times. I even had a photo, a silver gelatin print, given to me by a photographer. I had her book, too, with the same image on the cover, a flock of starlings transfixed in flight. I had seen them all, the birds, the sky, the field, the clouds, the utility poles, but I had not made any effort looking.

Seeing is by intuition. It doesn't take as much time as looking, I said.

How preposterous.

I'm only stating a fact about myself.

You can't understand poetry if you don't know how to look, he said.

That I agree with you, I said. I'm reading poetry these days. Isn't it interesting that I've begun to understand poetry now that I've begun to learn how to look?

Only you would find it interesting, he said. It's like someone saying, I only realize today eating is not a chore.

I laughed. Once upon a time I had been a careless cook. When Nikolai began to bake I gave up abstract-mindedness when making food. I used to think eating was a chore, he said to me after. Now you cook so well I understand why people like eating.

I'm rather dense, I said. Gormless, you know.

Dense and gormless were the favorite adjectives Nikolai and his brother used to describe me.

Do you really believe that?

Why not, I said.

How I always hate your hypocrisy, he said.

Oh, I said. I was taken aback. I was surprised that I had forgotten this: He had often called me a hypocrite when angry with me. I had never asked him what he meant by it.

You put on such an annoying act, he said.

Oh, what kind of act? I said.

Being dense and gormless.

What if I am? I said. I've told you, have I, that the character who resembles me the best is Winnie-the-Pooh.

That's called wishful thinking, he said.

What's wrong, I thought, with acting slow and dull if that makes people look away, or even, if they look, they can't see me, or only see me as a hapless bear with very little brain?

What's wrong with being sharp and bright? Nikolai said.

The world never tires of dimming the bright and blunting the sharp, I said. It's good to avoid suffering when one can.

So you play a dumb version of yourself, he said. Are you suffering any less?

Suffering, I thought, was a word that no longer held a definition in my dictionary.

But you, I said, you suffer more because you insist on being bright and sharp.

I suffer more because you want to do what the world does, to dim the bright and to blunt the sharp.

Why, Nikolai said after a long pause, you're quiet again.

Anything I say would sound defensive, I said.

Say it in any case, he said.

Had I been your age and had I been your friend I would have been bright and sharp with you. And I truly wish we had been friends. I love you so much but I can only love you as your mother. Sometimes a mother becomes the worst enemy because she can't be the best friend.

I love you so so much too, he said. I wish I didn't hurt you.

Oh, I said. I wouldn't say that at all. What's hurtful is life.

And it doesn't work when you act dense or gormless with life, does it?

No, I said. It blunts the sharp and the dull equally; it dims the bright but only makes the dim dimmer.

No need to act then? Nikolai asked.

Not anymore, I said.

5

Catchers in the Rain

Today's weather, I said, you would really like it.

Was there still weather for him, did he still feel it? It didn't matter. We used to often talk about weather, not as a substitute for real conversation, as weather was easily abused. Anything we had would continue to be ours.

Rainy? Nikolai said.

And gray and cold. Gloomy.

Precisely the weather I love, he said. I wish I could bake something.

A pumpkin pie would be perfect, I said. I didn't want to pause in case he and I both noticed that he had chosen the word wish. "To wish was to hope, and to hope was to expect"—I had once shown him the line Jane Austen used to describe the folly of two women.

Pumpkin pie? Too prosaic, he said. I would rather make pumpkin mochi.

Sounds like haiku, I said. I had forgotten the pumpkin mochi, which some of his friends, I now remembered him telling me, had looked at with suspicion at first but had relished after all. Baking had been a triumph of Nikolai's life when the results had been shared with friends. No matter how many batches of cookies and brownies and how many pies and cakes had been baked, someone would ask for more. Many of his friends had written to me, all of them mentioning his baking. Children are hungry on school days, I thought.

How patronizing, he said.

Oh, only because I just taught a story and I liked its title, "Children Are Bored on Sundays."

Children hate to be called children, he said. Besides, it's not about feeling hungry. The joy of baking and the joy of being baked for, you'll never understand.

I had long ago banished a few words from my dictionary: never, always, forever, words that equate one day to another, one moment to another. Time is capricious. To say never or always or forever is a childish way to reason with caprice.

Fine, Nikolai said. You don't care to understand— how about that? Good enough for you?

I used to get nervous on the days when he baked. Rarely was perfection achieved. A few times I had suggested that perhaps cooking would serve as a better—more forgiving—hobby. He had pointed out rightly that he couldn't possibly bring a platter of something that had had to sit overnight to the English class where they read Wilfred Owen or W. S. Merwin together.

Someone just sent a Merwin poem to me, I said. Since Nikolai's death I had asked people to send poems. They came like birds from different lands, each carrying its own mourning notes.

So?

I wondered if he still liked poetry.

Grownups make the same mistake over and over, he said. You like W. S. Merwin? What a coincidence—I just read a poem by him. You went to China this past summer? I did too, in 1987. Do you play any instrument? Oboe, how interesting, is that the instrument that looks like the other? Ah yes, clarinet! How wonderful you know exactly what I'm talking about.

Nikolai had a dislike for people who mistook the oboe for the clarinet. Not knowing is okay, he had once said, but pretending to know is not. How about I talk back and say, How interesting, sir, you must be Jones or Smith because you also have a head and four limbs.

I laughed. Critical as ever, I said.

I used to have this fear that when I grew up I would be like you, he said. I vowed to myself that I would never forget what it felt like to be a child.

You as me, your mother, or you as us, grownups?

Grownups as a species, he said. You're better than most.

Thank you.

That doesn't make you fundamentally different.

Disappointing all the same?

No offense, but yes.

I remembered my mother used to say: The salt a parent has eaten weighs more than the rice a child has eaten. Having lived longer . . . I said, not knowing where my thought was going.

Means little in the big scheme of things, Nikolai said.

I concur, I said. I had been listening to a song the day before—he had saved all his music on my phone, enough to last me days. *And don't you see I want my life to be something more than long,* I sang.

Sometimes you do make sense, he said.

It was silly how it made me happy, that little praise. We moved, I said, bringing up the topic I had not known how to broach with him. A week earlier we had moved out of the place we had rented temporarily and into a house with which Nikolai had fallen in love. Everything is good, except we miss you dearly, I said.

He became quiet. I realized that our exchange, however willfully sustained, was mere words. If he shed tears for us I would not have known. Tears we shed would be like weather to him, intelligible because they were concrete memories.

The kitchen is all set up and running, I said. It's warm and bright. It has the kind of oven you like. Perhaps I should start learning to bake.

That's nice, he said.

I couldn't tell if he was annoyed or bored or sad or angry. Tones were what we were missing now, and without tones words were floating, gravity-less, missing one another or, worse, clashing without a warning.

I wish I could show you the house, I said. I was treading dangerous water, but wasn't that what a mother should be doing, dreading the worst and hoping things would turn out better?

I have seen the house, he said.

With someone else's furniture staging someone else's life, I thought. Yet I shouldn't have had that thought. Nikolai had not relied on other people's furniture as placeholders. He had made plans for the kitchen and the garden and his bedroom.

Wouldn't it be nice if you lived in the house with us, too? I said, so softly that it was almost only a passing thought.

It doesn't matter, he said.

Why not?

It's still our house.

Ours, yes, but it was also a house of chutes and ladders, with empty walls and yet unpacked boxes making up the grids. Each box I opened let out memory that no space could contain. Each box that remained sealed retained its power to trip and trap. To throw or not to throw the dice: It makes little difference. In a game of luck, luck is already determined.

Since when have you become an avid consumer of inane analogies and inept metaphors? Nikolai said.

The adjectives you indulge yourself with, I complained.

At least I'm consistent. I've never said anything negative about adjectives. But you, you've been dismissive of analogies and metaphors.

I've started to understand the point of them, I said. They take up space, they distract, they make the difficult less difficult, they even fluff things up a little. And they can be a shortcut, too, the ladders, you know.

You're becoming a bad writer.

Does it matter? I said. I want a game with more ladders than chutes.

If you're protesting by becoming a bad writer, I would say it's highly unnecessary.

Dying is highly unnecessary too, I said.

Oh, people always die, sooner or later.

Always, ever, never, forever—had he lived to my age, would he have abolished these words, too?

There are plenty of bad writers, I said. What's so terrible about being one of them?

You sound like a child throwing a tantrum, he said. I don't get a chocolate. Why am I not getting a chocolate? It's so unfair I don't know how to button my coat anymore. It's so unfair I have to put my left shoe on my right foot and my right shoe on my left foot. And I have to stamp my feet until my toes hurt. And I have to punch the wall until my knuckles are bruised. And I have to shut my eyes so I will stumble and fall.

When I was a child, it was grownups who had the liberty to throw a tantrum, but this I did not tell Nikolai.

Still you don't get the chocolate, he said. Oh, poor, poor you.

You are not a mere piece of chocolate, I protested.

Why can't I be as daft as you and toss around metaphors and analogies?

By all means, please do, I said.

Then what? he asked.

I gave up. I was slow when we argued.

Then we become catchers in the rain.

Cold, wet, soles of our shoes slippery, our fingers numb, what could we catch? Any seasoned parent was an expert at catching: toppling babies, somersaulting spoons, half-eaten bananas and apples, half-ripe blood berries. Everything breakable and unbreakable belonged to a parent's field, but what could I catch on this gray, wet morning? Not the smile on your face, not the light in your eyes, not a blue cat, not a purple penguin, not dust in the wind, not a thought whispering in your ears, so loud that it had drowned out all the music of the world. What, my child, can I catch now, when all has become invisible?

Words, mother dear, Nikolai said. We will be catching each other's words, don't you see?

6

What a Fine Autumn

How are you today? I said. It was an inane question but I was too sad to look for a better opening.

Why don't people start a conversation by saying, Who are you today? Nikolai said. How anyone is matters less than who he is, don't you think?

Who are you, I said. It sounds intrusive, does it not?

How are you—is it less intrusive? If someone does want to know the answer it's intrusive too.

Who are you? I went over the question in my head. I suppose people would have a harder time saying who they are, truly, I said. Or there are so many possibilities it's hard to give one and neglect the other twenty.

When you see a tree, do you say, How are you today? Mediocre, the tree may think, because it's a windy day. But it's obliged to reply, I'm good, thank you, and you? No, when you see a tree you think, Here is a tree.

People are more complex than trees, I said.

We think we are, he said. So, who are you today?

I'm your mother.

See, you don't have a problem answering it right away.

But I wouldn't give the same reply if someone else asked me, I thought.

What if someone else did ask, Nikolai said. Say you go to a coffee shop and the guy at the counter says, Who are you?

I would say—I'm nobody.

How very imaginative.

But that's the problem, I said. Who are you is a question already asked and answered for us by a poet.

Dare we not make up a new and better answer?

Who are you? I said.

I'm somebody, he said, like nobody's business.

And nobody's fool, I said.

I'm somebody who's nobody's fault.

I wondered what the difference was between somebody and nobody. Any person with a solid physical form could not avoid having some body, which would make the statement I'm nobody a misclaimer.

Misclaimer for everyone but me. I can certainly claim that disclaimer. I'm nobody, he said. But I won't.

It was seven weeks since Nikolai had died. In Buddhist tradition, a soul leaves this world for the next after forty-nine days. I did not believe in this or the other world, the soulful or the soulless, the forty-nine-day gap where the departed retained their senses with an intensity that no living body could achieve. Still, what if he would not be here tomorrow? What if when I speak tomorrow, nobody replies?

That's silly, he said. Whether I'm here or anywhere is not decided by some tradition you don't even believe in.

Fear doesn't speak reason or logic, I said.

Phobia is irrational, he said. You *can* be reasonable and logical in your fears.

I counted my fears. Perhaps I should make a list of them and write the ways to be reasonable and logical next to each one.

What are days for me in any case? he said. Have you thought it may very well now be today and today and today and today?

I had thought about that. That, too, was my fear. Would one, plucked out of a timeline of yesterday and today and tomorrow, become a fish out of water?

A fish out of water, Nikolai said. Really, Mommy, the clichés you use these days, and not even to the point.

I would rather, I thought, have all the clichés in the world to make a tepid pond for myself.

So you could swim around like a sluggish koi fish? he said.

I protested at his unkind imagination.

A fish has only three seconds of memory, he said.

So you told me many times, I said.

Now that's called living in the moment.

I shuddered.

I know, he said. People say that all the time: You should live in the moment. Why, I used to want to ask, to live like a koi fish?

I must have been among the people who had said that to him, I thought.

Yes, you are, and I bet you ten dollars you don't even understand it yourself.

Five dollars? I asked. We used to bet on many things. Nikolai had collected a stack of IOUs from me.

Seven?

Okay, I said. You won. I don't understand it, and I don't believe it, either.

Are all parents expert equivocators?

I suppose the best among them are, I said. I'm not.

Why not? You're a good mother.

Not good enough to make you stay, I thought.

Well, I live in the moment now, he said.

In the moment: a life made of today and today and today and today. If that's all he has now, is it all I have, too?

If you don't mind my saying, what I have has nothing to do with what you have. Why put a bet on a nobody? You should make up your mind about what you want.

My mind is made up, I thought. It has always been. I want yesterday and today and tomorrow, all with Nikolai in it.

You often complain I want too much, he said.

Any parent would want what I want, I said.

Not necessarily.

Any reasonable parent.

Your argument doesn't stand, he said. A reasonable person can still want too much.

But a little more time, how can that be called too much? I said, though I knew I risked losing the argument. Are five years considered a little more in a lifetime? Ten?

Time is like money. Don't get into debt by spending what you don't have, he said.

I thought about the class he was to take in the spring, personal finance, which he had been looking forward to. What circumstance permits one to ask for tomorrow on trust?

None, he said. Time is a difficult debt to pay off. Impossible.

How do you know?

Because I've done that.

Did he mean that he had overdrafted his tomorrows? I remembered, when he was little, I had flinched whenever people called him precocious.

You kept saying, Be patient, he said. Many times I thought, Okay, let me believe you this once and wait, and things may change, and I may feel differently.

Most people do that, I said.

I suppose most people don't want to admit failure so they keep taking more credits from more tomorrows and get into deeper debt.

What if that is what people call patience? I said.

I wasn't a patient person. Neither was Nikolai. The root of patience comes from Latin, *to suffer* or *suffering*. What are other words that link pain to time, time to pain?

Nostalgia? Nikolai asked.

Nostalgia: *home* plus *pain*. Does he ever feel nostalgic, I thought.

I didn't leave home, Mommy, he said.

Still, I wish I had taught you how to postpone suffering.

If you haven't learned it yourself you can't teach me, he said.

A parent's folly, I thought, is to want to give a child what she does not have. A parent has to be quixotic. The word reminded me what I had forgotten all these weeks, that on the day Nikolai had died, when I had not known it would happen, I had been listening to *Don Quixote* on a long drive. I had been laughing to myself in the car. I had laughed at times since then, but that laughter in the car—quixotic—would never be mine again.

Are you not speaking because you've lost another argument? Nikolai asked. It was an odd relief that he would not see my tears. He had seen me cry only three times in his life.

No, just feeling sad, I said.

Still?

Still? I said. Sometimes I'm so sad I feel like a freak.

That sounds like self-pity unrestrained, he said.

I thought about my language. Indeed he was right. Not only was it immoderate but it was imprecise. How do you compare sadness that takes over like an erupted volcano to sadness that stays inside one, still as a stillborn baby? People talk about grief coming and going like waves, but I am not a breakwater, I am not a boat, I am not a statue left on a rocky shore, tested for its endurance.

Let me revise, I said. Sometimes sadness makes me unable to write.

Why write, he said, if you can feel?

What do you mean?

I always imagine writing is for people who don't want to feel or don't know how to.

And reading? I asked. Nikolai was a good reader.

For those who do.

For weeks I had not read well. I picked up books and put them down after a page or two, finding little to sustain me. I was writing, though, making up stories to talk with Nikolai. (Where else can we meet but in stories now?)

See my point? he said. You cannot *not* write. You don't even mind writing badly.

Because I don't want to feel sad or I don't know how to feel sad?

What's the difference? he said. Does a person commit suicide because he doesn't want to live, or doesn't know how to live?

I could say nothing.

I can always win an argument against you—do you notice that? he said.

Had I argued better, would he have stayed longer in this world? I didn't ask him the question. Like sadness, it was there all the time.

Instead I read him a poem I had translated from Chinese, one I had memorized when I turned twelve but only began to understand now.

When young, I knew not the taste of sorrow
But loved to climb the storied towers
I loved to climb the storied towers
To compose a new poem, faking sorrow

Now I have known the taste of sorrow
and want to talk about it, but I refrain
I want to talk about it, but refrain
And say merely: a chilly day, what a fine autumn

Is it a fine autumn? he asked.
Yes, I said. And a chilly day.

So Many Windows,
So Many Flowers

I wonder if I should start keeping a dream diary, I said.

The night before I had not slept well. When I woke up in the morning I knew Nikolai had been in my dream, but other than a mood, not a glimpse of time or place or his face remained.

If you want to, he said.

Did you like doing that? I asked. Nikolai had experimented with keeping a dream diary for a while. In a computer file, among many files that we had decided not to retrieve.

Marginally, he said. Why do you want to do it?

Why, I thought, isn't it obvious?

Not so to me, he said.

I told him that I wanted to remember the dreams in which he appeared.

Why do you want to remember them when you can talk with me? he said. Anyway your dreams are wishy-washy.

I had no doubt that what we had was realer than dreams. Still, it was only words we shared. We could not see each other. If a dream was kind it would grant what one wanted to see.

Dream on, he said.

In the past weeks I had seen him clearly only once—the other dreams, all like last night's, had fallen into the caprice of the human brain. A few days after he had died, in my dream we went to a hospital to pick him up. We waited where there was a compass on the floor, pointing to all four branches of the building, and we were there for a long time before we spotted him among people, many pushed around in wheelchairs. He was walking toward us, with an unhurried elegance that I often associated with a gray heron. But before he reached us I blinked and he vanished.

Oh gosh, Nikolai said.

What?

It's too neat, he said. A neat dream is all about self-indulgence.

Nikolai had been an early riser like me. Come here, Mommy, he used to call when he heard me up, in the same tone that had not changed between ages three and sixteen. I need my coffee, I often said, and I need my morning reading before I can talk. But he would insist, Come here, so I would sit on his bed, and he would wrap his comforter around, making himself into an eggroll. I had a dream last night, he would start. His dreams were about running, flying, teleporting, metamorphosing, but a few dreams had delighted or saddened me so much that I had recorded our conversations verbatim.

Here's one, from middle school:

I had an exhausting dream, he said the moment I sat down by him one morning. I dreamed that I was a negative number, and I couldn't figure out my square root.

It's possible, I said. Wait until you learn the imaginary number.

Mommy, I'm not stupid, he said. I know imaginary numbers, but I don't like to deal with that troublesome i.

(I had borrowed the dream to open a talk once. Nikolai had been proud of it, but his little brother, J., disapproved, saying the metaphor was too neat.)

Here's an earlier one. Nikolai was five, and one day

he told me a dream not from the night before, but from a few weeks earlier. It had taken him weeks to think about it before he could tell me:

I dreamed that you were driving the minivan uphill and you parked near Mari's house. Then you died, just sitting there. Many flowers fell onto the minivan and covered it. Then the whole thing became not so real-life, but like an oil painting. I woke up and cried for a long time and couldn't sleep.

Here's a recent one, less than two months before he died:

I dreamed last night we were traveling. We were going through security and a TSA agent said to J. and me: I'll be grading your conveying. And you snapped: Don't dandelize the dandelion.

What does that mean? I said.

I don't know, he said. In my dream I thought you made up the phrase on the spot to fight and you were pretty clever.

Don't dandelize the dandelion, I said now. I almost snapped at a student yesterday using the line.

Don't plagiarize my dream, Nikolai said.

I didn't. I gave her a stern lecture instead.

What snappable error did she make?

She said she didn't want to be serious, and she wanted to write fluffy stories so she could laugh at her characters.

What fluffy delusions a young person can afford, Nikolai said.

You're young, too, I said.

Not the way your student is young, he said.

What are your delusions like?

Does everyone have to have some delusion to live? he asked.

Does one have to have some delusion so as to be willing to die, I thought.

There's a fundamental difference, he said. You only die once.

So that's the end of the delusion?

Not in the sense that it disappears, he said, no. You still have it. Only it's no longer delusion but reality.

Is it not the case for the living? You treat the delusion as reality?

You don't meet your delusions when you're alive.

Like somewhere over the rainbow? I said.

Oh gosh, I thought, how I do think with words that are not mine these days.

It's okay, he said. You're forgiven.

I remembered an early spring day five years ago. I

took Nikolai and his brother to a seaside town, and after lunch we linked arms and sang all the way down the block, *We're off to see the Wizard, The wonderful Wizard of Oz.*

I remember that, Nikolai said. We must have looked so silly.

We looked happy, I said. It was off-season, and even adding up our ages, we still came below the average age of the local population. In the street, people smiled at our linked arms and choreographed steps, yet I was far from what they imagined. It was the year of my disintegration, and I could find few delusions to live for.

At least you make a point of appearing happy to everyone, he said.

You do, too.

I'm not as good at that as you are, he said.

His friends had written after, saying what a warm, cheerful, and happy person he had been in their eyes. A few had asked how they had missed his pain, what they could have done to save him. For some people a façade is necessary even with friends—especially so with those closest—but this I couldn't explain to the young, bruised hearts.

To live you have to propagate delusions, Nikolai said. One is not enough. A few are not.

How many are enough?

Are you asking me? You're the one living.

It's like asking the blind for directions, isn't it, I said, translating a Chinese saying for him.

Which, if you think about it, is nonsense. Who can say a blind person doesn't know the directions better?

Where should I go from here?

Oh you know you're doing fine.

I didn't know it. I wasn't feeling fine. I had but one delusion, which I held on to with all my willpower: We once gave Nikolai a life of flesh and blood; and I'm doing it over again, this time by words.

A good tactic is to diversify your delusions, he said. Don't keep all your eggs in one basket kind of thing.

I couldn't refrain from pointing out that he had used a cliché.

Whatever, he said.

Sorry, I said. Still, please enlighten me.

Oh, do what the squirrels do. Dig a hole and store a handful of delusions there, and dig another one and store more. Some delusions are for today. Some are for tomorrow. Some take a few months to ripen. Keep them dry so they don't get moldy. Keep them private so others don't step on them by accident or dig them up and steal them. Be patient. Delayed gratification is the key to a successful life of delusions. And if you're lucky, some delusions become self-seeded. Some even go wild like dandelions.

Are you making fun of me?

Indeed I am, he said. Nobody needs to be taught how to live under delusions. It's like sleeping.

There is a condition called insomnia, I said.

Insomniacs still sleep, he said.

Not efficiently, I said. Isn't it what insomniacs suffer, not having sleep of good quality? Barely hanging on?

As you've often discouraged me from pursuing perfection, I would say, Mommy, just do your best and stay contented with being a middling delusionist.

I wondered whether it was possible for anyone to be a middling delusionist. Seems to me, I said, a delusionist cannot take an adjective. You are one, or you are not.

Any noun can take an adjective if you know your grammar.

I tried to come up with examples to challenge his faith in adjectives. A procrastinating tree, a lofty shadow, an estival trance, a burdensome coda.

The ineffable miasma of incompetent words, he said. What do you call an aneurysm of a mind that's clotted by words?

As long as I stay clear of adjectives I remain uncluttered, I said.

Why such dislike of adjectives?

I oppose anything judgmental, I said, and adjectives are opinionated words. Happy, sad. Long, short. Live, dead. Young, old. Even the simplest adjective claims such entitlement to judge. Not to mention they come with those abusive forms of the comparative and the superlative.

I beg to differ, he said. A noun is a wall, an adjective is a window.

I laughed.

What's so funny?

There is no adjective in your astute and definitive statement, I said.

Fine. How about this: A noun is a self-defeating wall, an adjective is a tenacious window.

Self-defeating how? Tenacious how? I said. I was sitting next to a window, in the room that was called Nikolai's room. Outside were the procrastinating trees that had not shed their leaves as ordained by the season, which had made the gutter cleaners scratch their heads. In our old house in California we had large windows surrounded by trees that remained green all year round, and there Nikolai used to listen to Vivaldi's *Four Seasons* at night. In this new house there were definable seasons outside, but he would only have memories of the four seasons from music, not from experience.

Self-defeating as your mind is self-defeating, he said. Tenacious as my mind is tenacious.

Such immodesty, I said. My mind is not a closed room.

Mine has more windows, he said.

What is outside your windows?

All the good things you can't see.

Like what?

A garden of superlative adjectives. A path paved with lively adverbs. Poems without themes. Songs without names. There are ways to live not as a noun, or inside a noun, or among other nouns.

Yet it's all the nouns in the world that make room for the living, I thought. The living need the space within four walls.

What is outside your room? Nikolai asked.

I looked out of the window. Just the evening before, while cooking dinner, it had occurred to me that I could not open the window to pick a few bay leaves as I used to. Bay leaves came now in a little glass jar, sold on a shelf in a grocery store.

Flowers, I said, once the winter is over.

Well done, Mommy, he said. Flowers make a middling delusionist.

8

The Perfect Enemy

We baked a pumpkin pie yesterday, I said. Nikolai didn't speak right away, but I was certain he was listening. It wasn't as pretty as yours but it tasted good, I said.

It was the day after Thanksgiving. We as a family had never been good at celebrating. When Nikolai was in kindergarten, his teacher had had a conversation with me. We interviewed the kids, she said, and Nikolai said you celebrate many things but nothing seriously. Family tradition, she emphasized, is important for children.

Are some days more special than others, or are we giving them names and granting them meaning because days are indifferent, and we try to wrangle a little love out of them as we tend to do with uncaring people? These questions were not profound but they led to my halfheartedness about birthdays and major holidays.

The others—anniversaries, Mother's Day, Father's Day, Valentine's Day, a parade of holidays on the Chinese lunar calendar—were just that: days where we live.

Even so I had dreaded the first holiday without Nikolai. He used to bake around holidays. This time, I decided, we must make a pie ourselves.

He used to bake on weekends and on the days when he did not have much homework. He used to bake all the time, and how could we reproduce *all the time*? Butter and cream and honey and cinnamon and vanilla and nutmeg and clove and all the jars and bottles on his baking shelf: No one's words, Proust's included, could bring back to life their warm fragrance mixed with the scents of the winter rain of California and the wet eucalyptus leaves. You owe us an invention to immortalize scents, Mr. Edison. Without that our memory is incomplete.

At least the world is not inundated even more, Nikolai said. All the photographs and homemade videos. Imagine the Internet with smells and tastes.

The dead have the advantage of the leavers; those left behind have to have something to hold on to. But this I did not say. I should be the last one to make that argument. While unpacking after the move, I realized what a bad memory-keeper I was. School pictures from some years surfaced but not from other years.

An oversize album had only one page filled in, an ultrasound image of Nikolai when I was twenty-two weeks pregnant. The books in a complete set of *Tintin,* which had been Nikolai's favorite series in preschool, were scattered and not all recovered, as were those from the set of *Peanuts* that had accompanied us for years. The volumes I had found from the *Peanuts* collection were the ones he had been reading in the last days of his life.

There is never an end to what people want, I said.

If you want to be greedy, he said, make sure you're discerningly greedy.

We are who we are, I said. It was a hollow line, used often these days as though it could mitigate the pain in a hollowed-out heart.

Whatever that means, he said.

Nothing, I said. Saying something that means nothing is a skill you have yet to learn.

I'm glad I don't have to learn that, he said.

Saying something that meant nothing had become a new way for me to delude myself, as though something had changed. Nothing changed. Time stood still, for him and for us.

So you've settled in? he said.

Settled into what, I thought, days without him?

I mean the house.

We're like three little peas in a giant pod, I said.

The week before, I had explained to a friend that Nikolai could fill a space better than the rest of us combined. We had imagined a life in the house together, his cookies and cakes baking in the oven, his flowers blossoming in the garden, his music filling the house, his leaving and homecoming both cherished because what we had wanted most for him was the liberty to depart and the freedom to return. Mommy, I'm going to live with you until I turn seventy-three, he had said when he was three. No, no, I had said, you'll change your mind. Soon after, not yet four, he had changed his mind. I'm ready to move out, he had told me. No, no, I had said, you're still young.

There is no rule against anything, including settling into too empty a space, he said. Makes you feel organized.

Emptiness is different from unclutteredness, I said.

Clutter up then, he said. Clutter, clatter, clot, cluster.

None of the words, I thought, would release me from the void left by him.

You'll settle in sooner or later, even if it's against your wish, he said.

It occurred to me that I had never looked up the

etymology of the word settle, so I did. I read it to him: from Old English, *setlan,* from *setl,* seat—to seat, bring to rest, come to rest. Can parents' hearts find repose after the death of a child?

Perhaps I'm the one to ask the question, I said. Do you feel settled?

If you mean something sinking to the bottom, he said, yes, I feel quite settled. Sedimented.

What is it that's sedimented? I asked.

Everything about me that used to disturb me, he said. I'm all clear now, pure and perfect, just the way I want.

Nothing will come to disturb the sediments again?

What probability do you think there is for that to happen?

I did not know if I was sad or relieved, or sadder because I was relieved.

You see, this is your problem. When you don't have an expert command of adjectives, you don't know how you feel.

Perhaps I don't want to know, I said.

Why, then, are we talking?

I don't talk with you to figure out how I feel.

Why else? You're not going to say it's to keep me alive, that kind of nonsense?

I thought about a book called *This Real Night* by Rebecca West. For days and weeks after Nikolai's death I had often thought of the title. Since the moment I had learned of the news I had not had a moment of doubt about the coldest and darkest truth befalling us: This real night is and will be a permanent part of our life.

Fortunately for you and fortunately for me, I said, I don't believe in that nonsense.

Good, he said.

But J. and I are starting a memory book for you, I said.

Good grief, he said.

His psychologist recommended it, I said. I do think she has a point. Memories fade.

Why not allow the fadable to fade? he said.

Why not let the erasable be erased? I said.

Why not indeed? Everything in life fades or gets erased in any case.

I suppose you're right, I said.

Of course I'm right, he said. I'm so right I'm infallible.

For a moment I almost believed he was alive again, and I could hear him, his voice and his tone when he used to laugh at us, the fallible grownups.

Perhaps human history is driven by the desire to fight against our fadable and erasable fate, I said.

What pompous nonsense, he said. I hate it when you try to sound smart.

Well, we're starting the memory book in any case.

I can't stop you? he asked.

Just as I can't stop you from doing what you want to do.

Fine.

Not to make you more annoyed, I said, we have a perfect notebook for the project.

While I was unpacking I had found an old journal he had started at five, with a title "Sixty Years of Nikolai" written on the inside cover. He had kept it for less than two weeks, and had resumed with two entries when he was eleven, one starting with "Sorry it's been a long time!" and the second, four days after New Year's, "Sorry to be late! Happy new year!"

Oh gosh, he said. I remember that. Back then I thought a book had to have a title of some number of years of something, he said. All because of *A Thousand Years of Good Prayers*.

Sixty years of Nikolai, I thought. We only had sixteen of those sixty years. I was feeling sentimental. Numbers made me sentimental. Calendars made me sentimental. Things made me sentimental: a pair of sprinting spikes, a tennis racquet, sheet music on the music stand, a small acrylic painting of California golden poppies, a stuffed baby giraffe that had lost all its filling—I had sewn the tear back together but the giraffe remained skinny and floppy—a handmade print of a purple penguin with a bowler hat. Time made me sentimental: days and nights, minutes and hours, moments that threaten to become eternity.

What happens to sentimental when you take time out of it? Nikolai asked.

What?

You are left with gibberish.

What? I said. I was dense. Once Nikolai told me that J. had made an insulting joke about me: Mommy, you're dense. You're so dense if we put you next to a black hole, the black hole wouldn't suck you in but would be sucked in by you.

The word, Nikolai said. Did you notice *time* is in the middle of *sentimental*?

I looked up both words. Etymologically it means nothing, I said.

What an inelastic mind you have, he said. Do you really have to make this memory book? I can already see its quality. Embarrassing. Humiliating. Mortifying.

You could've written that book so much better, but I did not say it. There were many could'ves at this moment. I could go down any one of them like a path that led to nowhere, only to end up somewhere between doubt and regret. It was the maze I had decided not to set foot in. I would rather be here, hovering at the entrance, feeling and resisting the temptation of self-indulgence.

How I hate that word, self-indulgence, Nikolai said.

But I don't mean you. I've never called anyone self-indulgent but myself.

Isn't that a kind of self-indulgence, too?

Finding a self by negative traits is better than not having a solid self.

Even if the negative traits are imaginary?

Imagination is a kite flown by reality, I said. Imagination doesn't stand a chance if you cut the line held by reality.

Lofty, he said. Is that your secret?

My secret of what?

Of being you?

Do you mean being me as your mother, or being me, myself?

So there is a difference, he said. I often wondered.

One can stop being a parent or a child, a friend or

an enemy, one can stop being alive, but one's self does not stop being itself. Even death cannot change that. Death takes so many things away from us, but not that. Death is not invincible.

Are we not taking this self too seriously? Nikolai asked.

Of course we are, I said. We take it so seriously that even death, facing that self, pales.

How I hate this self, he said.

But you have a self that is . . . what is the adjective I should use? I said. Anything I could say would be a cliché.

Now is the time we have to be exact with verb tenses. Do I have a self? Did I? Will I?

A self is timeless, I said. Tenseless.

But it's flawed.

Tell me one person whose self is not flawed.

It doesn't work that way, Mommy. You know it doesn't.

You cannot demand that everyone be perfect.

I can forgive everyone, he said, for being imperfect.

But not yourself.

I tried, Mommy, I did try. Can't you see I'm perfect in only one way?

Perfect. Imperfect. A pair of adjectives that come

over and again, in all seasons, day in and day out, taunting us, judging us, isolating us, turning our isolation into illness. Is there a more accomplished adjective than perfect? Perfect is free from comparison, perfect rejects superlative. We can always be good, do better, try our best, but how perfect can we be before we can love ourselves and let others love us? And who, my dear child, has taken the word lovable out of your dictionary and mine, and replaced it with perfect?

I wish you had made me an enemy, I said, rather than yourself. Mothers, I thought, would be perfect for that role.

You can't be that for me, Mommy, Nikolai said. I've found a perfect enemy in myself.

9

Forever

I went to the car dealer today.

Did you say something? Nikolai said.

It was three o'clock in the afternoon, the most difficult time of the day. I was waiting for Nikolai's brother to come out of school. It took willpower not to turn around and look in the direction from which Nikolai would have walked toward me. I had willpower, but not enough at three o'clock in the afternoon. I waited in the middle of the block as though they would still have walked equal distances to reach me.

No, I didn't say anything, I replied. I was aware that I had been thinking of telling him about the car dealer. I had stopped right before the words had slipped out. It would have been small talk in another life but would not be the right conversation now. I did not want to become the kind of person recounting trifles to the dead.

We solved a mystery today, I said instead. Ever since we had moved into the house I had noticed a noise, rhythmic, seemingly coming from inside the house. I had thought it was a broken part of the heater. It turned out that a cardinal made a game of knocking on the basement window, knock knock, knock knock, with a tenacity. I've also seen it on the porch, I said. It's mesmerized by windows.

All birds are, he said.

But this one is persistent, I said. I wonder why.

I was still talking about trifles, but a befuddled and befuddling cardinal was more interesting than the car dealer.

It's just a bird, he said.

And a window, and a house, and a season, I said.

For sure you're not a connoisseur of nouns, he said.

A life's story can be told by the simplest nouns, I said. When I had first arrived in America, I would only buy white bread that was nineteen cents a bag. The next year, we upgraded the bread to twenty-nine cents a bag, and then forty-nine, sixty-nine, eighty-nine, until we had Nikolai and started to buy white bread at a dollar forty-nine a bag. I had never told him about the bread, or so many other stories. I had been cautious with the past, and wanted my children to live in a world where their parents' stories were boxed up and, if possible, sealed permanently.

Give me one example, he said.

Blueberries, I said. The first time we bought a six-ounce carton of blueberries, when you were three, it felt prodigal.

It's the adjective prodigal that tells the story, he said, not blueberries.

But prodigal wouldn't give me back memories of Nikolai as blueberries would. The summer before he had turned four, we had moved across the country to California, into a Spanish-style house on a college campus, with whitewashed walls, red roof, and a path in front of its picture windows, lined with eucalyptus trees. One day Nikolai and his babysitter took a walk and encountered a blueberry bush near the house. He picked some unripe blueberries, ate them, and ran all the way home, screaming and calling the blueberries ferocious.

I remember that, he said. I remember feeling smug because I knew the babysitter, what's her name, was impressed.

She also told me you called a tree theatrical, I said. How you do love your adjectives.

Yes, more than my blueberries, he said.

Is that possible? I asked. I had often joked that what other children his age spent on smartphones and games and outfits he had spent on blueberries. We used to store cartons of blueberries in the refrigerator and, when they were out of season, bags of frozen blueberries in the freezer. He ate his blueberries in a *Little Prince* mug I had bought for him in Paris, with a tiny silver spoon. No adjective could describe the mug, the spoon, and the last bag of frozen blueberries that we could not touch now. How long does it take for the frozen to become fossil?

I've begun to understand, I said, why people hold on to things.

I've begun to understand the opposite, he said. All things tangible, like all nouns, are dispensable.

What's indispensable then?

Adjectives.

That's questionable, I said. What's indispensable, really? I get confused with that question.

Nouns for most people, he said, because living in a world defined by nouns is obligatory.

I thought about his reply. Who can be free of nouns? Fathers, mothers, sons, daughters, friends, lovers, housing, food, career, retirement. We are brave children of braver parents, born into a web of nouns, and we are all like Charlotte, weaving a web for ourselves.

Except Charlotte chooses adjectives, Nikolai said, and she does it to save someone else.

Ah, I said.

You can't answer the question *What's indispensable* if you don't understand what's dispensable.

So the dispensable serve the indispensable, like the foundation of a pyramid and the pyramid itself?

That's a very bad analogy, he said.

Puissant, eupeptic, liminal, without nouns these adjectives of yours have little concrete meaning, I said.

The world would be a wilder place for imagination if you let adjectives go free without having to modify something, he said.

Imagination is a rubber ball, a dime apiece, I said.

What?

Oh, only a line I put in a recent story.

Rather facetious, isn't it?

What can be imagined, I wanted to say, is like what can be put into words. Nouns, verbs, adjectives, adverbs, pronouns, prepositions—it doesn't matter how many of them come together, they fall short together. I could imagine Nikolai arriving five minutes earlier than his brother, recounting the day while popping a cashew into his mouth now and then. I could imagine the confusion of our dog when I was unpacking and he was sniffing boxes with Nikolai's board games and books and a set of tools for making oboe reeds. Do you remember him, I had wanted to ask the dog, you, who have known him all your life? I could imagine rewinding life so I would again be making Nikolai's favorite dishes and watching him eat, or I would be listening to the conversation between him and his brother. I could imagine rewriting life so I would be buying tablecloths and cake pans and curtains and flowers with Nikolai. These imaginations made it easier for me to feel sad, to weep even, but the tears were a veneer over the unspeakable. It was what I could not imagine that made the veneer dispensable: the bad dreams he had not told me over the years, the steps he had walked and the thoughts he had gone through on his last day, the adjectives he would have taught me, the days and the years ahead—with or without him. The unspeakable is a wound that stays open always, always, and forever.

Oh gosh, he said. A wound open—that makes you sound like a mediocre self-help book.

Wouldn't a self-help book rather be talking about healing? I said. No self-help book would sell if it told you that the wound would stay open.

True, he said. Still, an open wound, what bad language you use now.

There is no good language when it comes to the unspeakable, I thought. There is no precision, no originality, no perfection.

Oh fine, he said, if you insist.

Fear not, I said. I would be the last person to write a self-help book.

Wouldn't a non-self-help book be more interesting?

A book about not helping oneself? I asked. A self-sabotaging book?

A book helping non-selves, he said. Like me.

It's not funny, I said.

It's only sensible, he said. If you're willing to read, you can find any number of books that claim to help you with grief or mourning or dealing with losses and traumas. There's no book helping me.

Helping you with what? I asked.

What's new to you is new to me too. How do I know what's a right way, or a good way, or a healthy way, or a mindful way to *be* now?

He had a point. Neither of us had any propensity toward religion or metaphysics. We had agreed to a conversation, sustained by my willfulness and his willingness. My willfulness, seen by the world as lunacy, might be pitied and forgiven, but my willfulness was also to believe in those who would not take this as insanity. His willingness was harder to read. Why stay present and sharp as though death had not left a smudge. . . . What if, I said, any way you are is a good way?

Sounds self-helpy, he said.

To think about it, perhaps there's nothing wrong with self-help. All selves need some help, I said.

Say, Nikolai said, if a self is seeking help, is it because it wants to be better at being itself, or being like others?

Oh, I said. I'm not an expert on that.

Imagine a self-help book wearing this blurb on the jacket: the secret to happiness—to be just like a million others.

Then a self-help book is to help a self to be better at being itself, I said.

Mathematically it doesn't make sense. How can a book help a million selves when each self is different?

So everyone has to have his or her own version. Each version bears a dedication: to my most precious self, which is unlike any other self.

Please don't be flippant, I said.

I'm trying to understand this as assiduously as you are.

I suppose it's like planting new trees. Each tree is unique, but to unfriendly nature and careless people all trees must look similar. A few universal stakes can help them stand.

I so hate it when you use analogies.

Is it really bad? I asked.

Unhelpful, he said. You talk about trees all the time.

These days my mind often wandered to trees. Is parenting not staking? We turn our torsos into determined wooden sticks, our arms into durable straps, and our hearts into gentle wraps around the young bark. We hold on to the saplings, vowing not to hurt them, hoping for their growth, but children are not trees. Sometimes they want to go their own ways—walking, running, flying—without feeling tethered. Children don't always put down their roots.

So much at stake, isn't it? Nikolai said.

Please don't make fun of me, I said. The question—what's at stake—was a perennial one in the classroom when my students discussed fiction. I had told Nikolai once that I had developed some allergic reaction to it.

All the same it would be much easier for parents to only raise trees, no? he said.

Even trees die, I said. I told him about a visit to a museum years ago, where I followed an arborist and the museum director around the garden. These trees here will die in about a hundred years, the arborist said in front of a grove, and explained that the museum should start thinking of replacements sooner rather than later.

A hundred years is a long time, Nikolai said. You wouldn't complain about not having enough time.

Losing a child, I said, has nothing to do with how much time a parent has already had.

Perhaps, Nikolai said. I feel bad for you. You really didn't think through everything before you had children.

There might not be any baby born if a parent were able to think ahead about everything, I said. Yet I wondered if that was true. Had I not for years been preparing myself for losing him, pre-living the pain, even?

Why did you have children, he asked, if you knew this might happen?

Even the least optimistic person wants to have some hope.

Wouldn't that be wishful thinking, the hope you talk about?

Possibly.

If you understand it as wishful thinking, why are you still sad then?

Why, I said. Because preparing is not experiencing. Pre-living is not living. I will be sad today and tomorrow, a week from now, a year from now. I will be sad forever.

I thought you said you took forever out of your dictionary.

Once upon a time, I said. You put it back for me.

A dictionary is not complete without the word forever, is it? Nikolai said.

All words are indispensable, don't you agree?

10

Waylaid by Facts

Your friend Martha wrote, I said.

She's in college now, Nikolai said. How is she?

I don't know. She didn't say in the letter. She talked only about you.

Oh.

I didn't recognize her name, but when she wrote that she was the bassoonist I remembered her, I said.

Poor Martha. I hope she has more time to practice now.

The girl had been in a chamber group with Nikolai the year before, and had been warned by the music teacher several times. Yet how could she have found time, trying to be everything she could and applying to colleges? At the concert last winter, she and Nikolai and a clarinetist played a trio piece by Bach. Halfway through she had slipped off and couldn't get back. She sat there, elegant in her long black dress and smiling at Nikolai and the clarinetist. Could you tell she missed the second part of the piece, Nikolai had asked, and when I said I couldn't he had been pleased. She played a few notes toward the end, he said, so it all looked as though that was what it should be like.

I had never talked with the girl but I was fond of that memory.

I wonder who else wrote you, Nikolai said.

Your friends, our friends, your teachers, parents of your classmates, people you don't know, I said. Oh, Lemony Snicket.

One thing I can't brag about now, he said. Which of my friends wrote?

Let me just make the turn first, I said. I was waiting for the green light, and I couldn't see much of the road. I had thirty minutes before teaching, and I did not know how my tears had begun between one block and the next. Something had ambushed me.

I still like waylay better, Nikolai said. Less seasonal than ambush.

What? I said.

Think, Mommy. It's winter. You're less likely to be ambushed.

I looked at the bushes along the road, bare and unable to hide anything. Try as I might, I still couldn't see many things seen by him.

Waylay is more inevitable, he said, unless you can avoid roads altogether.

The light changed and I turned into a street with old houses on both sides but no bushes. If you have a sudden possession of something you don't understand, I said, is there a way to discard it promptly without understanding it?

What is it?

Words provided to me—loss, grief, sorrow, bereavement, trauma—never seemed to be able to speak precisely of what was plaguing me. One can and must live with loss and grief and sorrow and bereavement. Together they frame this life, as solid as the ceiling and the floor and the walls and the doors. But there is something else, like a bird that flies away at the first sign of one's attention, or a cricket chirping in the dark, never settling close enough for one to tell from which corner the song comes.

If I could say what it is, I said, wouldn't that mean at least I have some understanding?

Do you understand a tree and how it feels when you know its name?

There are encyclopedias, I said. At least I can gather some general knowledge.

General knowledge is not going to help you, he said. But look at it this way: If you possess something, whatever it is, by definition that thing is at your disposal.

Yes, by definition.

Then dispose it!

How, I said, if I don't know what it is?

Isn't that what we have to do all the time? he said. You, I mean. Not me anymore. If you have a thousand dollars, it's easy to make up a plan about the money. But if you have a life, do you understand what a life is, do you know what to do with it?

A life is not a disposable thing, I protested.

When I say dispose it, I don't mean to get rid of it, but to settle it.

Oh.

There are better definitions for many words than the definitions you want to use, he said.

My dictionary is limited, I said.

No doubt, he said.

You know what I realized? I said. I don't want to use the word flawed anymore. I rather like limited.

A flawed character is limited, no? he said. I'm flawed, you're flawed, we all fault ourselves for being flawed.

A limited character, I said, may still be perfect.

You're not talking about yourself? he said.

Oh dear no, I said. Perfection is not my pursuit.

If you're talking about me, I can't make do with being limited and thinking of myself as perfect, he said. It is wrong from beginning to end.

My understanding is wrong?

Remember the Caterpillar said so to Alice?

Ah, yes, I said. A few years ago we had visited Alice's Shop in Oxford, and had brought two prints back, one with the Caterpillar telling Alice from on top of the mushroom, *It is wrong from beginning to end,* and the other, the Red Queen pulling Alice behind her and saying, *it takes all the running you can do, to keep in the same place.*

I've always found those two statements comforting, Nikolai said.

Me too, I said. Not always though. Sometimes.

On the other hand, he said, if we're willing, we can pick out any number of statements from any number of books and find them comforting.

Not for me, I said, not at this moment.

Why not? Don't you need more of those soothing words now?

I'm not looking for comfort food in any book.

What's wrong with comfort food? I like your little pancakes.

Little pancake was the name Nikolai had given to something I had improvised when he was in preschool. A simple mixture of flour, egg, sugar, and the key for them to be a genuine success was that every piece had its own shape, irregular, not representing any number, letter, or anything that could be pinned down by imagination. There were no two little pancakes alike as there were no two leaves alike. Dr. Seuss gave only twenty more letters on beyond zebra. I had cooked hundreds of them for Nikolai and his little brother. Like writing stories for only two readers.

What feeds your stomach should not be the same thing that feeds your mind, I said.

That belief is scientifically unsound, he said.

Yes, on the cellular level and on the molecular level, I'd agree with you, I said. Did I tell you about this man we visited for grief counseling? He asked us to imagine the universe as a giant cauldron of molecular soup. These molecules here make this table, those molecules there made Nikolai, I said, imitating the doctor, and began to laugh.

If he made you laugh wouldn't you consider him effective?

Upon our entering his office the man had also said, I sense suffering coming, but that I didn't tell Nikolai.

Some laughter does not last, I said.

Nothing does.

There are a few things that do.

Like what? Don't say love.

Our present conversation.

I noticed that you used an adjective, he said. Not our past conversations, or future conversations?

The word future is unnecessary if this conversation lasts, I said. Don't you think in this case futureless is not a bleak word at all?

How do you know this will last?

Indeed, I thought, how would I know?

And the past conversations? Nikolai asked.

They are memories.

And you don't think memories last?

One wishes they did, I said.

So memories are like cells, always replaced by new ones?

I thought about it. Without replacements would his

memories now remain unfaded and unfadable? Were they becoming part of his omniscience?

I've never thought about that, he said. They're not my concerns, you know?

I don't know, because I don't know what your concerns are these days, I said.

You used to know, he said.

Yes.

Why not anymore?

It'd be preposterous to say I know anything about you now, I said. I used to say one can know a person without understanding him, but I've never thought the opposite can be true, too, until now.

You understand me without knowing me? he asked.

Let's face it. Death is a divide no matter how little you and I believe its power to separate.

Is that how my friends feel too? That there is a divide between them and me?

A few of Nikolai's friends had written to him, remembering the time they had spent together, and asking why he had departed so abruptly. Others had written to us, remembering the time they had spent together, not asking what had made him depart so abruptly.

In some ways, I said, they don't feel that at all, but in other ways they feel it keenly.

I must point out a sentence like this is meaningless, Nikolai said. You can apply it to any situation to sound so profound.

For the record, I want you to know I've never used profound in my writing, I said.

Well, that is one adjective I wouldn't defend.

But I've been thinking about your friends' letters.

Don't make fun of their writing skills.

Nikolai's death was a difficult thing for people to talk about, but his friends, when they wrote, did not have to resort to the ready words because of helplessness, awkwardness, or politeness. They wrote from a place where Nikolai was still one of them and where they were told that he was no longer one of them.

If there is one thing to make fun of, I said, it's how quickly we grownups are at a loss for words in an unfamiliar or unwanted situation.

Unfamiliar or unwanted?

Sometimes it's hard to tell the difference.

An unfamiliar situation doesn't have to be unwanted, he said. Like love at first sight.

You're a true stickler.

You're the one to say precision, precision, precision.

What about this? We grownups quickly feel at a

loss for words when what words we have can't do half of what we want them to do.

Half, or a quarter?

We feel at a loss for words when they can't do fully what we want them to, I said.

They never can, Nikolai said.

Precisely.

Why not make do with the percentage they can achieve? he said.

Imagine writing a letter of condolence, I said, like this: I know my words are not enough to express my devastation at your loss and my words will not do much to alleviate your pain, but these words are all I have . . .

Sounds reasonable to me, Nikolai said.

I'm not done yet, I said. These words are all I have and we must make do with them, believing, both you and I, in the largesse in even such paucity.

So people are too modest to say that?

Or self-conscious, I said. Not knowing what to say. Not wanting to say the wrong thing perhaps.

What's the right thing to say?

There's no right thing or wrong thing to say in this situation. Your friends all seem to know what to say.

That's because they are *my* friends.

No, not only that. They are your friends, but they are young, too.

That's so ageist, he said. You should not hold it against anyone because he or she is young.

Rather the opposite, I said. What I'm trying to say is, we were young once. And your friends one day will grow up and become as gormless as we are. They will lose that one thing they have now.

What is it?

Your friends meet you where you are.

Where else can they meet me?

Yes, but think of what extraordinary courage they possess to meet you where you are. We grownups tend to get stuck with a fact, and for many people you have become a fact. Hard to accept. Impossible to understand. Still, you are a fact and that is how they will prefer to think of you and remember you now.

Not me, but my death, he said.

Important correction, my dear.

What do people do when they can't accept something they don't understand?

They ask, How could that happen? What went wrong? Or, they say things to the effect that in the direst situation there is a bright side if we let words like love and hope work their magic.

Does that bother you?

No.

Why not?

Because people who know you and people who know me meet us where we are. People who don't know you and people who don't know me are only facts. Flawed or limited, whichever adjective you prefer.

Just as we are flawed facts for them.

Exactly, I said.

Do facts meet then?

In fairy tales, I said, but not in this life.

Or in any life, Nikolai said.

11

Wishing You Were Somehow Here Again

Wishing you were somehow here again, wishing you were somehow near.

The line had been circling in my head. A little over a year ago I had lost a dear friend, and for days I had been listening to the song. *Help me say goodbye,* as though the departed had the wisdom, the courage, the inclination to lend a hand to us. Who helps them say goodbye? Not us, the living, limited by our living selves.

So many songs, like so many people. They come and go, or are never encountered. There must be a time in one's youth when real life seems to be in a thousand songs yet to be discovered, or another thousand songs destined to slip out of reach, not heeding one's wish to make them permanent. Does the shift come to all—or to some of us only—that the few songs that do stay, by fortune or by fate, are more prodigious than the whole world can offer?

I wish you were here today, I said.

You say that every day, Nikolai said.

I don't, I said.

You think that all the time, he said. If you don't say it aloud it's because you don't want to sound wimpy.

I don't want to sound wimpy, I said, and I'm not wimpy all the time. But I do wish you were here today. It's been snowing.

The snow, the first of the season, had begun in the morning. By late afternoon, the tiny prints of paws and the not-so-tiny prints of sneakers, left early on the patio by the dog and J., who had both seen snow falling for the first time, were covered again. For a while I had been sitting still, my chin cupped in my hands, my elbows on the table, watching the snow fall, until I realized that the pose was a reproduction of a famous still from a 1970s Taiwanese film, of a dreamy high school girl looking out of the window.

There is an idiom describing that, Nikolai said.

How strange and comforting, I thought, that my mind could wander but never far from his reach. Do you mean, mutton dressed as lamb? I said.

Yes. I always have trouble remembering it.

You lose nothing by not remembering it, I said. It's irreverent.

I like phrases of all kinds. I'm not as judgmental about words as I am about people.

It occurred to me then that the pose also belonged to Charles Bovary, who, with his chin in both hands, watched Emma with "stupid serenity."

Serenity is an overused word, Nikolai said.

Stupid is a necessary adjective here, I said.

I wonder if stupidity is one of the things that make the world go round, he said.

I hope not, I said.

We can argue about that, he said, but we will get nowhere. To think about it, stupid is a difficult word to use.

Why?

Because a three-year-old can use stupid correctly, he said.

Not so fast, I said. I happened to look up the word the other day. I encountered enough extreme stupidities for me not to investigate the word. Stupid, from Latin *stupidus,* be numbed, be astonished.

So?

So in a way the word is abused. It's deprived of its more feeling root, I said. Something happens, and it stuns us, it numbs us, it dulls us. There is much more sense and feeling involved in stupidity.

How about—Nikolai said—stupid sentences so afraid of tripping on an Oxford comma that they have to avoid it.

Oh, those poor sentences should not shoulder the blame for decisions they cannot control, I said. Nikolai was an adamant advocate for the Oxford comma.

Stupid yeast that goes on strike in scalded milk, he said.

I laughed. The first time he had made squash bread he had not waited for the milk to cool down before adding in the yeast. We had had a good laugh about the dough that refused to rise to the occasion.

Your turn, he said.

I didn't realize we were competing.

I thought for a moment. Stupid salt that thinks of itself as camouflaged snow, I said.

I won, he said.

Not really. The snow is so cold the salt is bound to feel benumbed, I said.

Benumbed, that was a word to describe myself all these weeks, benumbed yet un-astonished.

Stupid river that allows a stone to bounce on its surface, he said.

My heart ached. A few days before he had turned sixteen, I had brought Nikolai and two other children kayaking. It was a perfect afternoon, sunny, breezy, quiet on the river, the trees on both banks beginning to show the first hues of gold and red, a few dead branches floating along the canal. The children had been talking and singing and later taking a long hike along the tree-lined path, stopping now and then to skip stones. They had been confident in their happiness as the last days of the summer are confident in their everlastingness. While I was watching them, my heart had begun to ache with such vehemence that I had thought I was being assailed by a sudden illness.

You're only thinking back from a different place and adding your feelings, Nikolai said.

No, I protested. Some memories cannot be revised. They are what they are.

Fine, if you say so.

We were quiet for a moment. The snow, I said. You would have loved it.

Nikolai did not speak. The last time we had lived in a place with snow was more than twelve years ago. He was three, and with parental help had made a snowman thrice his height. I wondered if he had any recollection of the snowman.

Chopped down by two barbaric boys, he said.

Barbaric, I said, uncertain if that was the best adjective.

Used without any political connotation, he said. How sensitive people are these days. I speak from the point of view of a three-year-old.

It was true that the snowman had not lasted, born and destroyed on the same day. Two boys, seven or eight, had charged at it. Before we could rescue the snowman, its head was smashed, its body kicked around.

What else do you remember about that apartment?

Not much, he said. The playground. The red rock there.

Ah yes, I said. There had not been a red rock but he had cut his toe once, and bled so much that a rock turned red. In his confusion he had thought the red rock had done the mischief and all red rocks from then on were dangerous.

The apartment compound, of concrete and metal, used to be military barracks but by then served as inexpensive housing for graduate students and visiting scholars from around the world. Walk twenty minutes in one direction and one would meet cornfields. Ten minutes in another direction, a former campsite where thousands of Mormons, of English and Welsh descent, had begun their trek west, with near nothing but empty handcarts they had built for the migration—the city where we lived had been the end of the westbound railroad in 1865. Two hours' drive to the north was a house where Antonín Dvořák had spent a summer in 1893, composing *American Quartet*. The week before Nikolai's death he had been surprised that no one had recognized a Dvořák theme during an orchestra class.

Do you know Dvořák lost three children? I said. I only found out today.

I didn't know, he said.

When we said farewell to Nikolai, a dear friend played on her violin Dvořák's "Songs My Mother Taught Me." I had not taught him many songs, I had not told him many stories. But I had watched him live a rich life worthy of the songs and stories of the enduring kind.

Yikes, he said. Sounds like a bad sentence from a sentimental biography.

A parent should never be a child's biographer, I thought. How about, I said, you've lived a life with a richness both congruous and incongruous.

Congruous and incongruous with what? he said. How I hate your habit of using the opposite forms of the same word in one sentence. There is no precision. And no point to make whatsoever.

I flinched. When he was eight, he had shared a cab ride with an editor friend and criticized a story of mine she had published, explaining to her that she should have pressed me to work harder on the backstories.

Oh that, he said. I was giving you both a hard time because I just felt like it. Still, you need to know richness is an overused word, congruous or incongruous.

Intensity?

Equally bad.

Elegance, ingeniousness, perspicacity?

Gosh. Perhaps you should just stay with simple nouns like trees and flowers and leaves and birds and stars.

And snow, I said.

Yes, he said, why not?

Why not, I thought. Because a noun does not always remain a wall. Even the simplest noun can turn into a tunnel, a trapdoor, a maze, a vacuum, the Colosseum, the Great Wall of China, *Starry Night Over the Rhone,* the songs a mother has yet to teach a son, the stories a mother chooses not to tell. One can put one's trust in solid nouns—house, garage, road, breakfast, lunch, dinner, weekdays, weekends, holidays—as one can play the simplest tunes on the piano with a single finger. Twinkle twinkle little star, I'm a little teapot, Mary had a little lamb, Hey diddle diddle, but all of a sudden it's not an inexperienced finger picking out one note at a time but an uncontainable piece for four hands. Two strangers playing. One meticulously, the other recklessly; one exquisitely, the other mercilessly. Who are you? Are you improvising to entertain yourselves, or are you assigned to play this incongruous music called life?

What is music to life? Nikolai asked suddenly.

When Nikolai was in sixth grade, he had written a poem, remembered by my friends when they had come to say farewell to him, recited by his friends when they had said farewell to him on the other coast. I had put the first stanza among his photos in my office:

My life
is Kansas
and music

What is music to life? I said. You tell me.

Do you still have all those oboe recordings?

Yes, I said. His oboe teacher had given him recordings of several oboe masters.

When you listen to them, you realize how perfect they are, he said. I only wish I had played a single note as perfectly as they did.

I had not been able to listen to any of the recordings past a phrase. Any music with oboe in it was too much to bear.

You're still learning, I said.

Was, he said. I was learning. But this is what I've realized. Music can be perfect.

Life cannot be? I asked.

I don't mind that life is not perfect. I do mind that I cannot perfect myself in an imperfect life.

Perfection is like a single snowflake, I said. It melts.

A perfectionist melts too, Mommy.

12

Inertia

We bought a little tree yesterday, I said.

e. e. cummings's little tree? Nikolai said.

Goodness, I said, I forgot all about that.

So you just went out and bought a little tree for no good reason?

For Christmas, I said. Wouldn't that be a good enough reason?

No, he said. I thought you bought the tree because of the poem, and I was considering forgiving you.

In sixth grade Nikolai had chosen cummings's poem for an assignment. He was not often drawn to warmth and brightness in literature, and his commentary was as loving as the boy in the poem.

put up your little arms
and i'll give them all to you to hold

every finger shall have its ring

and there won't be a single place dark or

    unhappy

He speaks from a place dark and unhappy, you know? Nikolai said.

I know, I said. You also called the tree an orphan.

Did I? he asked. I don't remember.

Oh, you and I write about orphans often, I said.

And now you've made one more orphan out of a tree.

Orphan, widow, widower, I thought, but what do you call a parent who's lost a child, a sibling who's lost a sibling, a friend who's lost a friend?

I told you nouns are limited, Nikolai said.

Words are, I said.

Both Nikolai and his little brother had strongly opposed buying live trees, cut down to decorate a human holiday for a few weeks. We had kept an artificial tree, brought out every year along with ornaments we had begun to accumulate since Nikolai's first Christmas. But the tree had not moved with us, and we could not, I thought, go out and buy another one. The life of an artificial tree is devastatingly long.

Isn't that the point, to have something lasting, Nikolai said, instead of killing a tree each year?

It's a tiny tree, I said. More like a plant in a pot. Barely big enough for Alice after she shrinks herself.

A tiny tree is still a tree, he said.

We can keep it growing after the holiday, I said. It won't get dumped on the curb.

Whatever, he said.

Oh, judgmental as ever, I protested in my thought. And unforgiving. And unyielding.

Yieldingly and forgivingly I inquire, he said, Did you decorate it?

Thank you, I said. We did.

The day before, I had chosen five ornaments, the least weighty ones in our possession: a house, a snowman, a mitten, a penguin, two dog brothers sharing a stocking. The thin, supple branches held up well.

And presents, any little boxes under the little tree?

Only if they're the size of matchboxes, I said, but we can't put any presents in them. The moment I said it, a memory that was long gone resurfaced. Before I had learned to read, my father had saved used-up matchboxes for me. They had been versatile. I connected them into trains because I had never traveled on a train, I arranged them into sofas because I had seen sofas only in pictures, and I made fortresses out of them, following the war epics I had listened to on the wireless.

So, Nikolai said, they were like Legos?

Legos be damned! I said. The matchboxes were priceless.

Wobbly statement, he said. They were priceless only because your memory makes them so.

Okay. You're right.

Also, I don't like the word priceless.

It's an adjective, I said. I didn't want to say that I had learned the word from the television commercials for Mastercard when I had first arrived in America.

I know, I know, Nikolai said. But it's a derivative of a revolting noun. Like marrying a toad for unseemly gain. It comes at a price.

Everything comes at a price, can we not say that? I said. The flowers on the table, the photos in the frames, the stuffed penguins—forty-one of them—cuddled together, a livable life, an inevitable death, sorrow and stoicism, fear and despair. A self that, too close to one, does not stand self-injuring scrutiny; a self, too far removed, becomes a phantom limb.

Almost everything but one, he said. Time does not come at a price.

Sure it does.

You don't have to do anything for the minutes and hours and days to arrive, he said. You, meaning anyone living. You can't even stop time from coming at you.

It must go at a price then? I asked. Well spent, I thought. Misspent. If we don't have to earn our time, how easily we squander it.

Who's the judgmental one here? Nikolai said. Time you spend reading is as equally squandered as someone else's time spent playing Angry Birds.

In kindergarten he had once said that he wouldn't mind having a mother like his friend's mother, who sat at the kitchen counter playing Angry Birds.

And has it ever occurred to you that well-spent time is overrated? he asked. Well spent according to whom?

My time spent according to my own standard, I said.

How do you know your standard is not problematic?

I don't, I said. In fact, I think it may very well be problematic.

In what way?

I thought for a moment. When I was your age . . .

The worst way for a parent to start a topic, he said. As though people at the same age by default belong to the same species.

We do belong to the same species.

Don't be so literary, he said.

When I was sixteen, I said, I copied a saying from a Ming Dynasty book in my diary. The translation from Chinese goes like this, approximately: *If not for the frivolous, how does one manage to reach the other shore of life?*

In other words, if not for my famous frosting, how was I able to make a hundred and four dollars at the bake sale?

I laughed. His frosting had been an ongoing disagreement between us. The amount of sugar he had used had often made me cringe.

I made a resolution then that I should follow the advice from the old book, I said.

How did you lose your taste for the frivolous?

I didn't. What I thought of as frivolous turned out to be life, I said. My life.

Which is?

Reading.

Oh, that, Nikolai said.

In my time . . . I said. On second thought, I stopped.

I hope you're not going to speak like many parents. In our time, as though time bothers to make itself different for each generation.

Touché, I said. A purposeful life, when I grew up, had no place for poetry or fiction or philosophy or daydreams. Perhaps it's still the case. So you're right. How can I say my time is better spent reading than playing Angry Birds?

At least you're better at reading than at playing games, Nikolai said. And you're lucky.

How so?

Things you're good at may not treat you well in return, he said.

They didn't treat you well, did they, I said. Nikolai had been good at many things.

Being good is different from being perfect, he said.

Over and again we came to that adjective: perfect. Was there not one way out of its trap? Was there not anything—even something frivolous—that would have helped him reach the other shore safely?

I'm already at the other shore, he said.

People may look at it differently, I said.

They think of me as a shipwreck, don't they?

I did not speak.

They can think what they want, Nikolai said. People are afraid of death, people are afraid of the dead, and people are afraid of unusual decisions.

I wonder if fear is what keeps people going in life, I said.

Most people would say hope is a more suitable noun there, he said.

Who can tell the difference between hope and fear?

That's a good, muddleheaded question.

Oh, I remember another toy from my childhood, I said.

How nostalgic mothers can be, Nikolai said.

Though I didn't own it, I said. It was a spinning top that the big kids used to whip around in the courtyard. But even if you don't know what it looks like . . .

I do, Mommy. I'm not stupid. And I know you're going to use it as a bad analogy. You're going to say: We are the spinning tops, and fear whips us, and hope whips us, so fear and hope must be the same thing.

I thought for a moment. No, that's not what I meant to say.

Or you're going to say, Hope is the spinning top and fear whips it.

No, I said.

Fear is the spinning top and hope whips it.

No!

Then you're going to say the most refreshing thing—Fate, O Fate, O Fate, it's you who's whipping us! Nikolai said.

Stop putting words in my mouth! It doesn't matter who or what is whipping us, I said. Whatever it is, it's not doing that all the time. So my question is, What keeps us going then, fear or hope?

Scientifically speaking, it's rotational inertia, he said.

So hope is a kind of inertia? Fear too? I said.

Oh Mommy, you're getting so muddleheaded.

I'm muddleheaded, I thought, because I could go on thinking but would not reach any clarity: Which, between hope and fear, had made life unlivable for him?

I've never called life unlivable, he said. I've never lived a single day without something that matters to me, something that I live for.

But not a single day with just the frivolous?

What in my life would belong only to the frivolous?

Not music, I thought. Nor literature, nor sport, nor friendship. Baking? Cooking? Knitting? Gardening? Shopping for kitchenware, yarn, scarves, colorful socks? Choosing gifts for friends? Intensity makes frivolousness unattainable. Yet all those that have meanings have weight, too. Can a ship sail when it is loaded with what it is not equipped to carry?

I have sailed, he said, in my way.

Had there been a time when I should have known that what he called his way bode ill? When he, after watching the movie *Les Misérables* at twelve, had read the novel three times over the summer? Or even earlier, when his fourth grade teacher had sent me poems he had written, speaking of inconsolable bleakness?

Gosh, boding ill? I was only being me, he said.

Is it a fatal condition, I thought, for some people just being themselves?

And *Les Misérables,* he said. It makes me feel young again.

The novel was on his shelf now, with a small metal bust of Victor Hugo nearby. There was a collection of George Herbert's poetry, which he had picked out from my shelf around the same time as *Les Misérables,* yet to be studied. There were rolls of unknit yarn, volumes of untried recipes, years of unlived life.

Don't dwell upon the prefix, he said.

What?

You can add "un" to many words and undo yourself.

Undo, I thought. Undone. They were among the words that I did not say aloud, yet I had heard them used in connection to Nikolai. Even if people could refrain from saying them, these words were still not far, hovering with patience. Words are falcons, our minds the trainers.

No, our minds are the targets, he said, the prey.

Who trains the words then?

I don't know, he said.

I couldn't decide if the answer was an indication that he was losing interest, or he felt defeated. Perhaps the former, I thought. He had never given up an argument from defeat.

Undo is an overused word in any case, he said. You might as well say unfollow or unfriend.

Different, I said. You can easily unfollow or unfriend someone. You cannot undo many things in life. Most of life.

What can be unfollowed or unfriended doesn't matter, he said. These words, heaven knows they are really made-up words. They seemingly give you an option, but that option is not available when it comes to what you truly need to unfollow or unfriend.

Like what?

Death, he said.

If death cannot be unfriended or unfollowed, I said, shouldn't life be the same way?

I did not unfriend or unfollow life, Mommy. Had I done that you would not have found me. We would not have been talking.

What is it then you unfollowed and unfriended? I asked. If not life. If not death.

Time.

Time? I said.

Yes, time, which does not come at a price.

Unfriending it, unfollowing it, does it come at a price?

I don't know, Mommy. It's not for me to say.

13

Aftertime

I didn't get you presents for Christmas, I said.

It goes without saying, don't you think? Nikolai asked.

If it truly goes without saying, I said, I wouldn't have said it. It goes without saying—certain words are put together to say what they don't mean, or to mean what they don't say.

Trust me, he said. Every time someone says, Trust me, I want to ask, Why should I?

To be honest with you, I said.

With all due respect, he said.

I don't want to dismiss or diminish your struggle, I said.

How words waste space, he said.

Yes. And if I want I can go on and on.

A grownup is better at that than a child, no?

Yes, I said.

So, back to what requires saying. No present for me from Santa this year?

You've never believed in Santa.

I almost believed when I was little, he said.

When Nikolai was in preschool, he had once grilled me about how Santa could possibly visit all the children in one night.

I remember that, he said. You told me as long as I believed it, Santa would bring presents.

Did you believe then?

Not really, but I got my presents so I knew it was all made up, he said. I was worried for a few days. I worried that I would not get presents because I did not believe in Santa.

I didn't know these thoughts were going on in your head, I said.

It would be the end of a child's life had his parents known everything going on in his head, Nikolai said.

The next year I had received emails from several parents of his kindergarten classmates, alerting me that he had been spreading the news that there was no Santa. In our household we still follow the tradition, one mother wrote, and added that her daughter had come home with so many questions, including who eats the cookies and drinks the milk in the middle of the night, if not Santa.

So you enlightened me on the importance of keeping my friends in the dark, he said.

There's nothing wrong with parents wanting to prolong the childhood of their children, I said.

When I was in fourth grade I thought something must be wrong with my childhood, he said. It was too happy, never like what you read in literature.

I remember you saying that, I said. Is it parents' failure, I thought, if they've given their children a happy childhood that does not last?

A childhood ends, he said. Even the best parents can't change that. Sooner or later receiving Christmas presents is just for the sake of opening boxes. Inevitable is your favorite word for such things.

Sometimes you want inevitabilities to happen later rather than sooner, I said.

A mother we had met recently, who had lost a teenage son to suicide, had told us that every Christmas she would bring out his stocking with years of gifts, and she would add something new each year.

Don't do it, Nikolai said.

I'm not going to, I said.

I was not an organized person. The other day I realized I couldn't find Nikolai's stocking. Many things slipped away like sand or water, but did it matter?

Sand and water, Nikolai said.

I know, I said. Sometimes you can't avoid thinking in clichés.

They are clichés if you use them to describe time, he said. You're using it to describe a concrete object, which does not move itself.

Okay, I said, okay.

I'm sure the stocking is somewhere, he said. It can't be nowhere.

If you don't know the precise location of that somewhere, does it become nowhere? I asked.

It's still somewhere.

What do you call a place between somewhere and nowhere? I asked.

Between somewhere and nowhere—on some days that place feels more abysmal than on other days.

Anywhere between somewhere and nowhere would still be somewhere, he said.

Are you somewhere too?

Of course, he said. Nowhere is like infinity and beyond. It's possible to be closer if you try. It's impossible to arrive nowhere.

But it must be a somewhere different from this somewhere, I said. I mean, where I am. Here and now.

I was sitting in a room with books, and I was facing the window. On the windowsill was a vase of hydrangeas. A few minutes ago a woodpecker had been pecking a tree trunk nearby. And now a squirrel was digging with a frenzy, never pausing at a spot for more than two seconds. The weather for the next day, which was winter solstice, was forecasted as sunny. The year would end in ten days.

If it comforts you, I can make up something about my somewhere, he said. Here's a pond, yonder is the sky.

Just like the painting you did.

Which one?

When I was unpacking Nikolai's paintings, I had found one that I had not seen before. It had been done when he was much younger, as he had confidently misspelled his own name in capital letters on the canvas. There was the golden sky streaked with green, the red-golden field with an inset of an emerald-green pond, three brownish-golden barns towered by a golden and green tree twice the height of the barns. A child, taller than the tree, stood with a startled look on his face, his body the shape of a Christmas tree and decorated with golden ornaments, and on top of his head, instead of hair, he wore a bow tie the size of his entire body, purple with golden polka dots. Such an audacious and disturbed boy.

I remember the painting, Nikolai said. I hid it in my closet because I spelled my name wrong.

Everyone seeing it would wonder where that boy in the painting came from, I said. Or where that boy is now, I thought.

Somewhere, he said, but really, don't muddle your poor brain with riddles.

I told him the story of a dear friend of mine, who had been part of a lengthy program at a local music festival. By the time she was to play, it was late at night, and the music-saturated patrons had already crowded into the bar for reinforcement. When you play the piano to an empty room, does it still count as music? She and I had laughed on the phone about that question.

If you write poetry read by no one, does it still count as poetry, Nikolai said.

My heart ached. He had saved the music he had loved on my phone, all the way back to when he was six. It was a hodgepodge of classical music, Broadway musicals, lyrical arias, irreverent parodies of lyrical arias found on the Internet, soundtracks for video-games, and a folder of songs under "Edith Pilaf" (how we had laughed about his mistake). I was lucky to have every single piece of music he had listened to, yet luck in this story was purer and blinder than one could endure. Every time I turned on the music I thought of his poetry, written and yet to be written, unknown to me.

She herself heard the music, Nikolai said. That's the apotheosis of a musician's career, don't you agree?

Apotheosis, I said. I forgot you liked the word.

A noun too posh for your taste, he said.

A few years ago, when a friend had published the first two books of a trilogy, *The Apothecary* and *The Apprentices,* Nikolai had asked me to query the title of the third book. If she hasn't settled on one, he had said, I have a perfect title, *The Apotheosis.*

I still like that as a book title, he said.

I was going to give it to my children's book.

Oh that, he said. None of your characters would understand the word.

When Nikolai had turned five, I had promised him that I would write a children's book for him. Each year the promise extended to the next year. A few months before his death, I showed him the first two chapters, which he vehemently hated.

But Mommy, admit it, you can't write a children's book, he said now. You're bad at it. Dreadfully, frightfully, ghastly, hair-raisingly bad.

The adverbs you're addicted to, I said. I rather like the concept of the book.

The book, or what I had imagined it, was to be in part an autobiography of a rag doll that belonged to a little girl whose suffragette mother had been taken away to prison, and in part about the most impossible reader of the autobiography, a teenage girl living in the age of Snapchat and Instagram.

You could still write it, like your friend could play to the empty room.

No reason to write it ever again, I thought, if I had put it off year after year as though there were infinite time.

I thought you always prided yourself as a non-procrastinator, he said.

I've only procrastinated with that one project, I said. Many things, looked at from this side of death, gained bone-crushing weight. When Nikolai was in second grade, I had suggested that we eat out on the first day of spring break. Spring break is so short and I have so many things to do I cannot waste my life eating out, he had said. Oh, but a life is long, we have the time for a good meal, I had said. No, he had replied, there is never enough time in a life.

You can't do that, Nikolai said. Everything looks different if you look at it from aftertime.

Most things, I corrected him automatically.

If you insist on being so annoyingly precise.

Is aftertime a word? I asked.

I think so, he said, if there is noon and there is afternoon.

Word and afterword, I said.

Math and aftermath, he said.

Life and afterlife, I said.

None of them sounds as appealing as aftertime, don't you think?

But are you sure you are using it correctly?

Oh what does it matter, Mommy? Any moment that comes after time is aftertime.

Are we in aftertime then? I asked.

I am, but not you, he said.

Why not me?

You've said you live in days, so you are still in time. You can't live in aftertime.

I remembered an older German woman, who had been Nikolai's favorite preschool teacher. I had often thought of her as the most optimistic and efficient woman, calm and with good humor among three- and four-year-olds, all of them clamorous and demanding. She had once joked that her only contribution to America was to have adopted our family for Thanksgiving, an American holiday.

She taught me to play Nine Men's Morris, Nikolai said.

Yes, I said. I found the board the other day.

Just wish I could see him again. When you come back please call me so we can cry together. I am so sad, the preschool teacher had written from California. *I thought we prepared him to live.*

She did a good job, Nikolai said. She taught me to garden and make cheese crisps and baked apples.

She also taught you that song we loved.

The little donkey song?

Yes, I said. The first time Nikolai had sung it at home, I had felt tears heavy behind my eyelids.

If I had a donkey
That wouldn't go.
Do you think I'd beat him?
Oh, no, no!
I'd put him in a barn,
And give him some corn,

The best little donkey
That ever was born!

How ignorant and happy I was beforetime, Nikolai
said.
Is beforetime a word?
As good a word as aftertime.

14

Consolation

I made a cake for Christmas Eve, I said.

Was it a success? Nikolai said.

Half of a success, I said. I made a Japanese cotton cheesecake. It's a nice-looking cake, cheesy but not cottony.

So you failed the other half, he said. Now you understand my frustration as a baker.

Yes, but it's okay. Sometimes the first draft of a story doesn't turn out right.

Except you forget a cake is a one-draft story. You don't get to revise.

But to rewrite? I said. I'm going to try again. Baking can't be harder than writing, don't you think?

You still don't get it, Mommy. You can't go back to make the cake twice. Like you can't step into the same river twice.

Just as none of us could go back, re-measuring the ingredients that made up days and years, repeating the steps with more care, hoping to eliminate the errors, hoping not to make new mistakes, so that this story would have turned out differently. And Nikolai would still be alive.

I thought we were discussing baking, he said. Don't make any unnecessary leaps.

One doesn't, I thought, have to make a leap at all, when every time one looks up from a book or turns around in the kitchen or fills a vase with water, one bumps into that monumental absence.

Monumental? How clumsy, how cumbersome, how unwieldy you make me feel.

How you resort to redundancy to make a point, I said.

I know, he said. But really, monumental is a deathly word.

A friend of Nikolai's had written, reminiscing that when they stood in a circle to talk, he bounced up and down as though he had springs in his shoes. Another friend had told me that when they had gone out for walks, he would jump into the air to pick the plums that were out of everyone's reach. A mother of his classmate had written, telling me that he would always remain in her memory as the boy who had raced his friends down a street lit up by orange lights on an autumn night. How can one make a monument, granite or marble or bronze, lithe and nimble in flight?

I would say a cotton cheesecake is a more sensible quest than a monument, Nikolai said.

I told him that the word monument came from Latin *monumentum,* memorial, and *monēre,* to remind. I had looked it up, along with mind and memory and mourn. Many words had to be relearned since his death.

Do you need a monument to remember me? I would rather you were reminded of me by a piece of cheesecake.

Because you're a baker, not an architect?

Because cheesecake is perishable, he said.

Oh, I said. I've never used perishable in my writing.

Better than that word you never tire of using, inevitable.

They are different adjectives.

I prefer a world made of the perishable, he said. Not the inevitable.

Inevitable makes time more bearable, I thought.

Time doesn't make sense if not for the perishable, he said.

Okay, I said. We can have different opinions.

As long as you promise not to use monumental again, he said. You really need to sharpen your skills with adjectives.

I had a dream last night, I said, changing the subject. In my dream I was going to pick up Daddy and J. from a hotel, which was like the hotel we stayed at in London.

Were you driving?

I parked the car nearby.

You can't drive in England, he said. You don't know how to drive on the left side.

Oh it was a dream, I said. At the hotel entrance all of a sudden you were walking next to me.

In my dream Nikolai was wearing his favorite blue-striped T-shirt. Mommy, I'm hungry, he said to me. The moment I heard him I woke up. Before reality and un-reality were separated like night and day, darkness and lightness, I lived over and again with his smile and his voice in my head.

I wish I could tell you I had had the same dream, Nikolai said. Then it would feel like it truly happened, no?

I thought about several people who had told me their dreams about the departed. Often the dreams were interpreted as signs of communication from the other world. Yet dreams are but prologue to days, epilogue to other days, written by our faltering minds.

It would be a terror, I said. People with their independent lives should not meet as independent entities in dreams, too.

Even when one of them is no longer alive?

That changes nothing about an independent life already lived, I said.

But then it's unfair, Nikolai said. How do you know if someone wants to be in your dream?

Like how do I know you would rather be playing hide-and-seek with me at night than telling me you were hungry? I said. Alas, I don't know. No one has a choice when others decide to capture him or her in their dreams.

So fundamentally dreaming is injustice inflicted upon whomever is being dreamed of?

Sometimes self-inflicted injustice, I said. People you want nothing to do with still come into your dreams.

Just like baking then, he said.

I thought baking was the opposite of dreaming, I said. You have a precise recipe, with everything in control, and you get the right product in the end.

Did you get everything in good control when you made the cheesecake?

No, but that was because I'm not an Able Baker Charlie as you are, I said.

Bad pun, he said.

What?

ABC, he said. American Born Chinese. You should know my friends and I never use the term.

Oh, I said. It's never occurred to me. I only thought of Able Baker Charlie from Richard Scarry.

When Nikolai was little, I was fascinated by a Richard Scarry book, *What Do People Do All Day?* Once, while having an official coffee with a dean at a university where I used to teach, and not being able to decipher her words, which were seemingly pregnant with meanings, I blurted out without thinking: What do you do all day?

I've noticed that you like to ask people about what they do for a living, Nikolai said.

For a living, yes, but that's a compromise, I said. What I really want to ask is: What do you do *all day*?

How meddlesome, how intrusive, how impertinent.

If days are where we live, I thought, I will always want to know how people live in their days.

Why? he said.

Don't you sometimes have the feeling that others have answers to questions you don't have answers to?

But others may look at you and think the same, he said. What if I ask you, What do you do all day?

Oh the things you know, I said. Reading. Writing. Cooking. Looking out of the window. What do you do all day?

Oh the things you don't know, he said. Dreaming. Dreaming. Thinking. Dreaming.

What do you dream about? What do you think about?

Not telling.

Oh, I said, okay.

We were quiet. I thought about the dream from the night before. There were old recipes I no longer cooked because they had been his favorites. There were new dishes I had made since. It was hard enough when a child said he was suffering and a parent could do little to help. It was beyond helplessness when a parent could do nothing to mitigate a child's hunger.

Be careful, he said. Don't overinterpret anything. I'm not hungry. You only dreamed of it.

Do you still suffer? I said.

That's a worse question than What do you do all

day, Nikolai said. Imagine greeting someone. Hello, nice to meet you. Do you suffer?

You're the one who says we shouldn't ask inane questions, I said. Do you still suffer?

He was quiet for a moment. Depends how you use the word, he said.

I looked up the word suffer. It comes from *sub,* from below, and *ferre,* to bear.

So, if you ask me whether I still have to bear the weight of living, he said, no, I don't suffer anymore.

What do you have to bear? I said.

Things that are always with me, with or without a physical body, he said.

I rearranged a vase of half-withered hydrangeas on the windowsill. Sometimes when I felt agitated I walked from room to room. Each room was full of objects, still lifes in his new home. Still life, still part of this life. For years he had asked me: If you write about suffering, if you understand suffering, why did you give me a life? I had never given him an answer good enough.

Now we're both sad, he said. We're good at making each other sad.

I thought I was better at making you angry, I said.

True, he said. We do argue a lot, don't we?

All the arguments we had, looked at from this side

of death, had been about a promise a mother could barely deliver, and a wish that the child suspected would not come true. Often I had told him, Life is difficult but things will work out in the end, as long as we have patience. Patience, patience, he had said. Do you really think everything will be better someday, when I'm older?

I'm not mad at you anymore, he said.

I know, I said.

All those storms—I had thought we had weathered them together. But perhaps there is no true togetherness when some pains remain incomprehensible.

Oh, I forgot, I said. I did learn one thing when I was baking the cake. I figured out how to make the parchment paper stand in place.

How? he asked.

A few times when Nikolai made cakes, he and I had struggled to make the parchment paper stay upright in a perfect circle while he poured the batter in.

If only I could show him, I thought. Not telling, I said.

Come on, he said. There are a million things worth not-telling, but not a little trick in baking.

There are a million things worth living for, I thought, including a little trick in baking.

You don't even believe it yourself, he said.

What if we don't have to believe anything, I said. Perhaps living only requires resolutions.

Like New Year's resolutions? I thought their whole point is not to last?

No.

Like finding an answer, a solution? You're bad at giving answers, but I've found mine already.

Like resolving time: a year into days, a day into hours, an hour into minutes, I said.

But has it occurred to you that time thus broken down makes quicksand? he said.

Yes, I'm fully aware of that, I said.

And you still resolve to live on quicksand?

What you call quicksand, I said, is our reality.

Yours and mine?

Yes, our genes.

Why don't we get to live like other people, on flat and solid earth before it was discovered to be round?

Other people live on other kinds of quicksand, I said.

Really?

I don't know, but I like to imagine that is the case.

I don't think so, he said. What's underneath the quicksand?

What's underneath? I said. I don't know.

We don't fall into an abyss for no reason, he said.

What if, I thought, we keep trying? What if an abyss can be made into a natural habitat? What if we accept suffering as we do our hair or eye colors? What if, having lived through a dark and bleak time, a parent can convince a child that what we need is not a light that will lead us somewhere, but the resolution to be nowhere, even if it's ever and forever.

What then? he asked. That I would make do with my imperfections ever and forever?

No one is perfect, I said.

That's an old line, he said. It means nothing to me.

Life is imperfect, but it does mean something, no?

Yes, it's a consolation prize, he said. But I don't live for consolation prizes, Mother dear.

15

Never Twice

It's that time of the year, I said. I'm thinking about my New Year's resolutions.

Do you remember last year's resolutions, or the year before last's? Nikolai said.

If I go back and look for them in my journal, I said. Ha.

But I'm still making a list.

Let me see, he said. You're going to bake a lot of cakes.

How do you know? I said.

Because I know how unimaginative you can be, he said. If you said horseback riding or beer-brewing or beekeeping or stargazing, I might not have guessed.

It doesn't bother you, my taking up baking?

What do you think? Baking is my territory, he said. Cooking is yours.

But you are learning to cook, too, I said. I was keenly aware that we were both using present tense.

Baking is my meditation, he said.

I know, I said. He used to bake when he was agitated.

What is baking to you? You can't meditate my meditation, he said.

Remembrance, I thought.

Baking doesn't allow revision, don't forget, he said.

Knitting does, I said.

You're going to knit too?

When I was a small child, I had been trained to knit every summer, with old yarn that had already lost its elasticity. I had hated the rusty-red stringy yarn, scratchy on my sweating arms. I had hated that my mother would examine my work at the end of the day. And I had hated, most of all, that after the ball of yarn was used up I had to unravel it and start all over again. But these things I had never told him. The first time he discovered that I could knit he had been impressed.

Only because you don't look like a knitter at all, he said.

Why not?

We knitters find joy and comfort in repetition, he said. Can you write the same sentence over and over?

What if life requires a certain amount of repetition, I said. I can't write the same sentence or story over and over, but maybe I can use knitting to meet the requirement.

At least you're better at knitting than baking, he said. It's possible for you to knit and achieve something even if you can't, like any self-help book would advise you, enjoy the process.

Thank you for your rare praise.

Remember the octopus you knitted? he asked.

I had almost forgotten. In middle school, for Secret Santa, Nikolai had asked me to knit an octopus. Two days, he had said. No way, I had said. Yes way, he had insisted. By the end of the two days I had given him an octopus, which had an opal-white body, light-blue tentacles, and beady eyes that did not match in color or size. The next day he had come home and demanded seven more octopuses for friends.

Octopi, he said now. I hate when people say octopuses.

Fine, octopi, I said. Etymologically we're equally right on this.

Octopi sounds more erudite, he said. So you're considering starting to knit again?

I did knit a little.

When?

Oh, a while ago, I said. For days and weeks after Nikolai's death, I had spent much of my time in his room, knitting, unraveling, knitting, unraveling.

Which yarn did you use?

The canary-yellow.

What did you make?

Nothing.

What were you planning to knit before you made nothing?

I thought I would knit a scarf like you did, I said, but I kept messing up my counts and starting all over.

Nikolai had knitted several scarves. He had worn them in Tibet when he had visited there in the summer, and had planned to wear them this winter, too.

Sometimes you can revise as much as you want, but it still doesn't come out right, he said. Which can make knitting worse than baking.

Your scarves all came out so nicely.

That's because I'm good at counting, he said.

I helped, didn't I? I said. He used to shout random numbers for me to remember. I still had series of numbers typed in my phone.

I don't think you're good enough to put those numbers to use, he said.

So should I put knitting on my list of New Year's resolutions? I said.

I would say if you include both knitting and baking, that would be overly sentimental, he said. I expect more of you than that.

What about music? I asked.

Gosh, you're too old to learn oboe!

Not oboe, I said. Piano.

So someday you can play Für Elise?

There was a time in my childhood when our doorbell and the doorbells of the two neighbors' apartments all played Für Elise in the worst rendition, like old musical greeting cards running out of battery. I can't stand that piece, I said.

I know, he said. Many piano students have to play it, so that prospect, let's hope, will discourage you from piano.

Maybe I can go back to my accordion.

That's a good thought, he said. You can even go to a pub to play. Loud and cheery. With some rouge and a bohemian flair.

How you make a point to oppose every pursuit of mine.

I'm only being realistic and responsible, he said, so you don't fail by January tenth.

I bought a dictionary for myself, I said. And it's my resolution to study it every day.

Because you need to brush up on your vocabulary to be on par with me?

A Dictionary of the English Language, I read to him, by Samuel Johnson.

Okay.

You said okay because you don't know who Dr. Johnson was, I said.

Dr. Who? he said. Oh fine, I don't know.

There was no joy, however, in having scored a small point. There were so many things I wished he could get to know and love someday. A week before his death he had told me he was looking forward to studying *Macbeth* in English. Once in a while I had asked him to give *War and Peace* another try—he had read a hundred pages in seventh grade, and had reported having understood nothing. Later I realized that he had been unaware of the fact that the dialogues in French had English translations in the footnotes. Who reads the footnotes when the book is already so thick? he had protested. A friend had read a Wallace Stevens poem at Nikolai's memorial, but it was not a single Stevens poem, but all his poems, the work of a lifetime, that reminded me once and again of Nikolai. A mind that sees no path or direction to flee despair can be expanded nevertheless. Who can say if expansion may not one day make despair sufferable? I wished I could still leave some books on his desk, a Wallace Stevens collection among them.

Oh don't wish, he said. Wishing only wounds the heart.

What's the harm of spending a few minutes lost in wishing, I thought, when the deepest wound would remain open, day and night.

Then find some distractions, he said. Wishing is not a good way to distract yourself.

I read him a quote from Marianne Moore. "If nothing charms us or sustains us (and we are getting food and fresh air) it is for us to say, 'If not now, later,' and not mope." Often I had gone back to the quote, saying to myself, If not now, later.

I never mope, Nikolai said, if you haven't noticed.

Of course I have, I said.

His joy and his suffering, neither in minor key, precluded moping. Yet what if, I thought, moping is a bridge to reach Moore's later?

There is no later, he said. For some people it's now and now and now and now.

Tell me about it, I thought. It was exactly three

months since his death. Seasons have changed. All lives in nature have changed themselves, as ordained by the seasons. It's later and later and later and later for them, helpless as they are to want to make permanent any kind of now. A dear friend says we only count days and weeks and months with this intensity for two reasons: after a baby's birth, and after a loved one's death. Three months feel as long as forever, yet as short as a single moment when it's now and now and now and now, so I must tell my friend that there is a difference between life and death. A newborn grows by hour, by day, by week. The death of a child does not grow a minute older.

Does this count as moping? Nikolai asked.

What?

Your going over useless thoughts.

Useless according to whom? I snapped.

Sometimes you sound like me, he said. Very un-Mommy-like.

Sometimes you sound like me, I said.

What a terror, he said. No child likes to detect any trace of his parents in himself.

Not even the good things? I asked.

When bad things have to come along, too? he said.

A few times Nikolai had commented that he had

got the mathematics and science genes from his father, talent with language and good work ethic from his mother, music and sport and a sense of humor from himself, admiration from his little brother—yet it was so rare that he could look at himself that way. Contentment was never a word in his dictionary.

Sometimes, I said, only sometimes, I do think you have a point in questioning why parents give children lives.

Why do they in any case?

Blind hope, I said, or wishful thinking.

See, you're moping now.

No, this is not moping. I don't mope, either, if you haven't noticed.

Okay, I'll give you that, he said.

Yet what if moping is the exact thing that is needed for those who don't mope, I thought. One doesn't kill oneself while moping.

I would say stick with any virtue or vice that you can't change, he said. If you're a migrant bird you can't be flightless. If you're a flightless bird you can't leave New Zealand.

Or Australia? I said.

Any island, he said.

We never did visit Australia together, I said. Remember Rosie?

Rosie had grown up on an Australian farm, and had visited us when she was five. J. was six, and Nikolai was nine. The day she left, walking up the driveway of our old house, she had turned around with tears in her eyes and waved at the boys. Come visit me soon, she had shouted at them. Don't wait till we're old.

You can't go back to every little memory and cry, Mommy.

How do you know I'm crying?

Because Rosie represents the quintessential neverlastingness of good old time.

Quintessential, I said. Do you know it shares a root with Quintus?

Quintus had joined the household when he had been nine weeks old. Nikolai had been the one to name the dog *The Fifth* in Latin, after the four human beings in the family.

Nikolai did not speak. Did he miss Quintus?

You can't step into the same river twice, he said.

Sometimes once is hard enough, I said. I admire you for having done that, and you have done more beautifully than many people I know.

Oh Mommy, don't make it sound like an elegy.

No, it's not an elegy, I thought. No parent should write a child's elegy.

Don't be so sad, he said. Don't mope.

Can I read you a poem? I said.

If that makes you feel better.

So I read him a poem by Wallace Stevens.

This Solitude of Cataracts

He never felt twice the same about the flecked
    river,
Which kept flowing and never the same way
    twice, flowing

Through many places, as if it stood still in one,
Fixed like a lake on which the wild ducks
    fluttered,

Ruffling its common reflections, thought-like
    Monadnocks.
There seemed to be an apostrophe that was not
    spoken.

There was so much that was real that was not
    real at all.
He wanted to feel the same way over and over.

He wanted the river to go on flowing the same
    way,
To keep on flowing. He wanted to walk beside it,

Under the buttonwoods, beneath a moon nailed
    fast.
He wanted his heart to stop beating and his mind
    to rest

In a permanent realization, without any wild
    ducks
Or mountains that were not mountains, just to
    know how it would be,

Just to know how it would feel, released from
    destruction,
To be a bronze man breathing under archaic
    lapis,

Without the oscillations of planetary pass-pass,
Breathing his bronzen breath at the azury centre
    of time.

16

Answers Do Not Fly Around

I've gone back to Shakespeare, I said.

I didn't know you stopped, Nikolai said.

He wouldn't have known. A little over a year ago, the day after the presidential election, I told him that every morning, I would read Shakespeare's work before I made breakfast for them, and I would read his plays in chronological order, once, twice, however many rounds allowed by four years. I had stopped the morning after Nikolai died. The last morning we had had—I still remembered the giant volume opened on the dining table when he had come out of his bedroom. I remembered every single word we had exchanged until he exited my car near school.

Every single word? he asked.

Yes.

How can you be certain?

Because there had been eight hours of uncertainty, during which I had re-lived that morning, moment by moment, but this I didn't say. Remember when we were in Ireland, you chastised me because I ordered the food in the same accent the waitress used? I said. You thought it sounded like I was mocking her?

That's a non sequitur, Nikolai said. I would believe it if you said you remembered some of the things we said to each other, but everything? Every word?

When I turned ten, I said, I made a resolution to memorize more poems than anyone in my life would have read. I kept the habit until I was in my twenties.

Now we're in parallel conversations, he said.

What I'm trying to explain is this: Some people live by images, some by sounds. It's words for me. Words said to me. Words not meant for me but picked up by me in any case. Words in their written form. Words that make sense and words that make nonsense.

So your brain is like a flypaper for words.

Gosh, I wish you could unsay it, I said. Now I'll always feel a little disturbed by my brain.

LOL, he said.

I did not speak. As far as we were separated, I could still hear him. When he had first begun to adopt Internet slang, for a long time I had thought LOL meant "Lots of

Love" and had cherished it when he said that to me. The misunderstanding, once cleared, had given Nikolai and J. a good time laughing at my gormlessness.

Remember the flypapers we saw in the Summer Palace? Nikolai asked.

It was on a smoggy morning a little over a year ago when we had gone to the Summer Palace. The sun had been an orange, metallic disc next to a high-rise when we left the hotel. From there I could retrace the course of the day, of boating and walking and playing word games and counting the flypapers around the lake all the way to a conversation with a cabdriver, who explained to me at length what it must mean for me to live in America and how I must parent my children with their Chinese roots. Too many people ready to offer expertise on things they knew nothing about, I had thought then, like too many cars congesting the traffic.

I remember that, Nikolai said. I was eavesdropping on your conversation. I was feeling bad for you.

Nikolai was a good eavesdropper. Eavesdropping used to be a crime, I said.

I know, he said. I've been to your talk on eavesdropping more than once. Writing fiction is to eavesdrop on your characters' hearts.

It occurred to me, when he said that, that I would not give another talk on eavesdropping again.

Why not?

You can't carry everything from one life to the next, I said.

But why leave the good things behind? he said. I rather liked listening to you talk about eavesdropping.

More of a reason to leave it with you, I thought, just as I had sent him off with a silk scarf of mine, intense with blue and yellow, of Vincent van Gogh's *Starry Night*. The scarf had been my favorite, and his, too.

Steal-listening, he said. An act of theft. Do you realize if I want I can do that even better now?

No doubt it's the case, I thought. When was the last time you performed the act? I said.

At that lunch with your friend, remember?

I did not have to ask him the question to know that was the last time. On that day he had had a copy of *Great Expectations* open in front of him, but when my friend and I began a disagreement, he could not contain his smile. What were we arguing about? I said.

She asked you, in your imagination, what you wanted your novel to be. You said the main character outlived everyone so it was a book about the kindest revenge. She said that sounded cruel, and you said there was no cruelty, as the character had done nothing hurtful but to live on.

At that moment we had both turned to Nikolai, knowing he had been listening. What is your opinion, asked my friend, showing him the definition of the word *revenge:* to avenge by retaliating, to inflict injury in return for. And he had confirmed that yes, any revenge would be cruel.

You remember things well, I said.

If you can brag about your memory, why can't I?

Things we remembered together, things we remembered differently, and things we remembered separately. Later that day I had taken him and his friend to the Empire State Building in a storm. They had run around the observation deck in the whipping rain. I had taken a picture of the city before the evening lights lit the streets, the sky heavy with grayness, the city gray with concrete buildings, except for the golden pyramid on top of the New York Life Building. Shall we change the subject? I said. I could remember and remember and cry and remember.

You started this whole catching-every-word-with-sticky-memory-paper conversation, he said.

I did, didn't I? Will the memory paper catch words yet to be said?

Like this year's flypapers catching next year's flies before they are born? Like the White Queen saying memory works both ways?

Oh, I forgot the White Queen's claim, I said.

If you and I can talk, he said, nothing is impossible.

Yet someday, I thought, people would question these conversations between him and me. Insanity or religiosity, some may say, or both.

Is that really your worry? he asked.

No.

Then why would you even spend a second thinking about it?

Oh, a mind catches a thought here and there too like flypaper, I said. Besides . . .

Besides what?

Nothing.

You can't stop a sentence in the middle, he said. At least keep thinking to the end so I know.

Besides, I thought, someday I may have to face the question of protectiveness.

Protective of yourself?

No, I said.

Me?

Yes.

Me? he said. Me? Mommy, you know that should

be the last of your concerns. Me, needing anyone's protection now? No, no, no. People say that about the dead, that they need to be protected, only because people need an excuse for their own timidity.

How so?

Because they don't know what the dead want. And they're afraid of knowing, Nikolai said.

They're afraid of not knowing, too, I said.

Are you?

Of knowing or not knowing? I'm not afraid of knowing.

Then you're afraid of not knowing?

Yes, I said. Sometimes. A little.

You can ask me.

That, I thought, was my fear. Whatever questions I asked I had to answer for him. The world we shared was limited, even if our words were not.

What if I surprise you with an answer you wouldn't have thought of? he asked.

Shall we try?

Only do not ask stupid questions, he said.

Like, What did you have for breakfast?

Or, Do you regret what you did? he said. Do you miss being alive?

I remembered the science fair when he had been in

third grade. A parent had hailed us across the room. What are you doing there, Nikolai? He, standing next to his poster, had looked perplexed. I'm . . . uh . . . living, he had replied.

I forgot about that, he said. But it proves my point. Don't ask self-evident questions.

Is there regret in his world now? Nostalgia? If they were self-evident I did not know the answers. I had not thought of asking him. Should it have occurred to me that these were legitimate questions?

Thank goodness you've spared both of us those questions, he said. What do you want to ask then?

I told him about a meeting we had had with another mother, who had lost her son six years ago to suicide. She was a woman with strong convictions, one being that her son and Nikolai had already met in heaven, and they had meant for her and us to meet in this life.

Oh my, he said. Is that what you wanted to ask, if I've been to heaven and made a few friends with backgrounds that are similar—not culturally, not ethnically, not socioeconomically—what's the right modifier here?

Please be serious and respect where other people come from, I said.

Yes, yes, yes, he said. As long as you don't imagine a heaven for me.

One of Nikolai's friends had read a poem for him at his memorial, ending with a stanza: *I am an atheist / but if one person can change that / it is you, Nikolai.* I told him about the poem.

I don't want to change anyone, he said. I don't want anyone to change because of me.

That, I'm afraid, is not for you to decide.

Fine. But you have to know she was only writing a poem. Just as you're writing stories here.

Yes, I said, but poems and stories are trying to speak what can't be spoken.

You always say words fall short, he said.

Words fall short, yes, but sometimes their shadows can reach the unspeakable.

Words don't have shadows, Mommy. They live on the page, in a two-dimensional world.

Still, we look for some depth in words when we can't find it in the three-dimensional world, no?

You look for it, do you mean? I don't look for anything now, he said.

Yet he had indulged me in this world of ours, made by words.

What I wanted to ask you, I said, is this: How long can our conversation last?

Can? I thought it was for you to decide. I didn't make this happen. You did.

I did, didn't I?

So the question is for yourself, he said. How long do you mean for the conversation to last?

Tomorrow, the day after tomorrow, ever after, forever, but none of these, I thought, is the right answer. There would be the time when he would have turned seventeen, eighteen, twenty, twenty-six, thirty, thirty-six. Days where he ought to have lived but will never again. It would be an error to keep him forever at sixteen. Now, later, then, and then.

You write fiction, Nikolai said.

Yes.

Then you can make up whatever you want.

One never makes up things in fiction, I said. One has to live there as one has to live here.

Here is where you are, not where I am. I am in fiction, he said. I am fiction now.

Then where you are is there, which is also where I live.

Wouldn't that be confusing? he said.

Did I tell you I returned to the novel? I said.

The one you talked about at that lunch?

Yes, I said.

Another world you have to live in.

Yes.

That's one book I won't be able to read, he said.

That's one book you don't have to read, I said.

In the novel a woman lost her child to suicide when she was forty-four. I had not known the same thing would happen to me when I was forty-four. There were many other things I had not known when I had been working on the novel.

Agh, now people will blame me, Nikolai said. When you publish the novel people will think you've given the woman that story because of me.

People can think what they want, I said.

Maybe you've been writing the novel to prepare yourself, he said.

I have been writing to prepare myself my entire career, I thought.

Where do you think this conversation is going? I said.

You ask how long it goes, and where it goes, he said. The questions you ask are the ones you should have answers to.

Time points only in one direction. A mind goes in

many directions. How far digressed are we allowed to
be on a one-way road before we are called lost? And if
one is not lost, can one be found again?

Answers don't fly around like words, I said.

Questions do, right? he said.

Indeed they do, I said.